Harbor

by

The Sea

W. M. ANDREWS

Sparrow Ink
www.sparrowink.com

Stay in touch with W. M. Andrews
and all her upcoming publishing news.

Sign up for her biweekly newsletter

No one talks about what happens
when happily ever after goes wrong...

Fall in love, get married, have babies.
It was a simple dream.

Evelyn accomplished the first two easily.
She almost had it all.

Almost.

But after three years of
aggressive fertility treatments, all she had to show
for her efforts was a broken heart and a painful rift
in her marriage. She'd hoped that a
dream vacation to the south of France would heal
her *and* her relationship with her husband.

Then Eric suggested she go alone, and she started
to question *everything.*

Did he want a divorce? Or did he just need a break
from their shared grief? Evelyn wasn't sure. All she
knew was that if she wanted to find a way to
reconnect with Eric, she had to learn to
love *herself* again.

And what better place to do that than a harbor by
the sea?

**Harbor by the Sea is a sweet, angsty, romantic,
contemporary women's fiction read about hope,
the importance of finding one's own joy, and
the enduring power of love. Download today and
get ready to root for Evelyn and Eric's second
chance romance.**

*This women's friendship fiction book will bring you
all the feels. If you love women's fiction with a side
of clean romance, this is a great fit for you.*

~~~~
~~~~

Acknowledgements

My first acknowledgment has to go to my awesome, supportive husband. Without his easy-going nature and technical assistance, my books would never make it to publication.

Rebecca, a dear friend and beta reader, gave me invaluable feedback when I struggled in the murky middle. Without her help, this book never would have made it!

Editors are every author's most important partners and this book was blessed with two – Emily Clark and Julie Sherwood. If you find any mistakes in this book, those are entirely the author's fault.

My gorgeous cover is thanks to Les at GermanCreative.

Dedication

Evelyn struggles, it seems, with nearly everything. She has tried too hard to shove herself into all the boxes expected of her. Now she's reached a certain age where some decisions are no longer in her hands and finally she's angry. This leads her on a journey of discovery to figure out what's truly important to her. If you're on a similar journey, this book's for you. You'll get there.

XO

Chapter One

"**W**ell, isn't this romantic?"

Evelyn McConnell could hear the sarcasm dripping from her words. Sarcasm wasn't her. Or so she thought. There were a lot of things she'd thought about herself that were proving to be untrue. She had thought she'd be a mother by now. Even though she told herself she had accepted her infertility, just thinking about it filled her with sorrow and anger that threatened to swamp her. That was the biggest mistaken thought of her life. She'd thought her husband would always be by her side, but he wasn't here. And she'd thought she didn't have a negative bone in her body.

And yet here she was in Nice on her romantic trip of a lifetime. Alone. Childless and alone. And, apparently, feeling a little salty about it.

"It is, in fact."

Evelyn nearly expired from the embarrassment. She had quite forgotten that people could hear her. Just because she couldn't understand most of what was being said around her didn't mean no one could understand her. She ought to remember that when she was talking to herself. Before the embarrassment actually killed her, Evelyn mustered up a reply. As a former executive assistant, she could manage composure in most any situation.

"I'm sorry, I was talking to myself."

"Often the best companion you're going to find," the man said with a grin and a wink. "I'm Carl," he added. "Where are you from?"

Heat started to climb in Evelyn's chest. She hoped she didn't blush right in front of this handsome stranger. He probably wasn't flirting with her. It was ridiculous to even think that. He looked to be at least five years younger than her, for starters, and in excellent shape. Not to insult herself, but she would readily admit that she hadn't taken the very best care of herself in recent years. If she were to glance at her reflection right now, she would see a very tired thirty-eight-year-old woman with dishwater hair and eyes that might be green or blue, depending on the light.

She used to look after herself though. Perhaps the man was just a very practiced flirt. A part of her thrilled at the thought of a good-looking man flirting with her. The rest of her rejected the thought.

"My husband and I are from the east coast of the United States."

"Ah, a husband. *Desolé*. But then, you see, it is romantic, *n'est-ce pas*?"

It would be if Eric were here, Evelyn thought, but she couldn't say that to the French Flirt. That thought brought a contrary amusement to the fore.

Evelyn gestured out the window toward the gorgeous pebble beach and the turquoise sea. "Nothing could possibly be more romantic."

This time she managed to keep the sarcasm from her tone and her smile pleasantly neutral. She might be mad at her husband for letting her come all the way to France by herself, but she wasn't about to complicate matters by encouraging a stranger to flirt with her.

Her discouragement tactics seemed to have worked. After a jaunty nod and a smile to her, Evelyn watched with wry amusement as the man turned and found someone else to dally with.

Evelyn turned back to her own concerns. In a foreign country, alone. How was that for romance and togetherness? She and her husband were supposed to be on this trip reconnecting after their headlong pursuit of parenthood had driven a wedge between them. And what about her safety? Didn't he care about her safety at all? She'd never done anything alone in her entire life.

But of course, as he'd said, she was a "highly capable woman."

"It will be good for you."

Evelyn had stared at him.

"Good for me? How will going to a foreign country, all by myself, be good for me?"

At first, she had been more confused than angry, but when he'd said that going alone would be good for her, she had wanted to yell and swear. But she wasn't the sort to do either, so she had managed to swallow down most of her feelings. Remembering how she had remained calm in the face of Eric's outlandish statements made her wonder if she were due for a prize. Any woman told by her husband that going on a month-long, international, dream vacation without him would be good for her deserved a medal if she managed not to commit violence upon his person.

Good for her, my patoot. How was being in a foreign country with a foreign language and culture all by herself supposed to be good for her? Was that in the vein of what doesn't kill you makes you stronger?

At least he had known it was important to her. He had acknowledged that.

"You've been dreaming of seeing the Mediterranean for as long as I've known you. Even if I can't be there, I know you'll still love it." He had sounded reasonable, but Evelyn could barely hear him above the ringing in her ears.

Maybe she was just cranky from jetlag. That's what Evelyn tried to tell herself, anyway, as she glanced uneasily around the tiny little café she was sitting in *by herself* feeling completely conspicuous even though no one was really looking at her. It was beautiful despite its diminutive size. Evelyn was beginning to realize that was true of everything in Nice. Small and gorgeous. But it would be even better if Eric were there.

Take a deep breath, Evie. Evelyn could almost hear her good friend and neighbor, Rachel, say the words in her ear, and she tried to obey them. Evelyn didn't do breathing exercises and affirmations like some of her friends did. She had never thought she had the need. She thought her life was bordering on perfect. All they'd needed was a baby to complete it. But things were definitely changing. A couple deep breaths later, and the waiter finally brought the beverage she'd ordered along with the pastry her thighs didn't need. And as she savored the buttery, flaky goodness of her croissant, she immediately began to feel better.

Café au lait. That was the closest thing she could find to what she was used to drinking—a coffee with cream. It looked delicious despite being the smallest cup of coffee she'd ever seen in her life. The croissant was bigger, and seeing that lightened her spirit, causing a giggle to threaten to overtake her.

If she didn't want to be conspicuous by sitting alone in a café, she better not start laughing by herself, she thought with another inward roll of the eyes followed by a soft sigh.

Maybe she had just been hungry. Flying through the night, losing six hours from time zone changes, and not really sleeping, would mess up a person's inner rhythms for sure. This little, well not so little from the looks of the croissant, snack would set her to rights again.

It wasn't Eric's fault he wasn't with her. He had a work emergency. Well. She maybe needed to grow a back bone. She didn't need to turn into an angry, sarcastic person, but it *was* his fault. He worked for himself. She was pretty sure he did investments. While he usually went into a big office in the city for his work, surely it was something that could be done online. And if it could be done online, Evelyn was pretty sure even in the south of France they had the internet.

Again with the sarcasm. But this time she kind of liked it. She needed to start standing up for herself, at least within her own thoughts. If Eric was going to send her off on their romantic trip of a lifetime by herself, she was going to make it transformative.

She thought back once again to the moment he had told her he wasn't going. No one had actually forced her to go alone. On that score, she only had herself to blame.

"I think you should still go."

Evelyn looked up from the pile of laundry she was sorting. She'd been absorbed in her own thoughts, as usual, and couldn't fathom what he was talking about. Had she missed part of the conversation?

"I beg your pardon?" A frown of confusion creased her forehead.

"You should go on the trip without me."

Her frown deepened and she turned fully toward him, blinking. "Why would I do that? I'm sorry, I don't understand what you're saying."

"Everything is already booked; it wouldn't be fair for you to miss out."

"Am I having a brain aneurism?" she had asked, hoping a joke would lighten the moment. "Why would I miss out? Did you tell me something that I've forgotten?"

Evelyn was genuinely confused. Was she losing her mind? "Are you saying you aren't going?"

"Yeah," Eric said with a deep sigh as though he were very put upon. "Something serious has come up at work. I can't go. But you've put so much work into planning the trip. I think it would be really good for you. You should still go."

Evelyn stared at her husband, unsure how to react to what he was telling her. "I really don't understand this, Eric. We've been planning it for weeks. Of course, we're going. I don't think I could actually cancel it at this point. Certainly not with a full refund."

"Exactly, that's why I think you should still go." *His gentle emphasis on the "you" filled her with a bleak feeling.*

Every emotion chased itself through her. Evelyn couldn't decide if she were devastated or furious. But she didn't give vent to any of her feelings. She just swallowed them with a gulp and nodded.

Thinking about it in hindsight, she should have told him how she truly felt, about everything, but especially about the idea of going on their dream trip alone. But, as usual, she had been a pushover, not wanting to stir up any controversy with him. Which was foolish. She loved her husband. And he loved her. Didn't he?

"*Will you still be able to drive me to the airport, do you think? Or should I arrange a taxi? And will you cancel your flight? That's really the only element that is affected, I suppose. I will still need the apartment."* She was babbling about the practicalities instead of the actual issue. "*I can do that for you, if you'd like. I probably should. That way I can make sure my flight isn't affected, since I bought them together."* If she didn't take care of the details, she was likely to fall apart. How could he cancel their dream trip that she had spent the last three months obsessively planning, and untold years dreaming about?

"Of course, I'll drive you. Thank you for understanding. And yeah, it would be great if you could take care of the flight for me."

"At this point, they might only give you a voucher for another flight," she warned. "But I guess that will be better than losing out completely."

Eric sighed again as though she were burdening him. "I know, it's a waste but it can't be helped. I'm sorry."

He didn't really sound sorry to Evelyn, but she didn't call him out on it. What could she say anyway? If he didn't want to go, he didn't want to go. She understood his work was important and people relied on him. Emergencies did happen. But she thought he'd made arrangements for the time away. Couldn't whoever he'd arranged to stand in for him look after the emergency? If there really was an emergency. She didn't know how to ask him about it without sounding like she was making inappropriate accusations. They didn't do that in their marriage. She didn't want to start now. But the accusations floated through her head anyway.

Evelyn resumed sorting the laundry. It wasn't going to wash itself. But now she didn't have to be too rushed over Eric's. If he wasn't going to come with her on their planned dream trip, she didn't have to give too much thought to his clothes. He wouldn't be packing any, it would seem.

Was steam coming out of her ears? She was angry enough at the moment that it was just within the realm of possibility.

Just thinking about it now as she took a sip from her ridiculously small coffee cup, even though that was days ago, made anger well up into her chest once again. How could he have thought it was okay to send his overly sheltered, rather clueless wife, off to a foreign country for a month without him? Did he hope she was going to get killed? Would that simplify his life? Then he could find a wife who was able to carry a child for him.

She tried to get out of her head and turned her eyes outside of the café. The glint of the sunshine off the turquoise blue waves was almost blinding. But in a good way. Was blinding ever good? It had to be when it was the Mediterranean. Eve brought her focus inland, closer to the café. As luck would have it, a mom walked by following a laughing toddler, who appeared delighted that she was allowed to walk by herself.

Emotion cramped Evelyn's chest. The toddler looked to be about three—the age their child would be if they had been able to get pregnant when they'd first started trying in earnest.

Eric had so deeply wanted a biological child. She did, too, of course, but somehow biology had failed them. Eric would be better off if she didn't make it home from this trip. Or perhaps he just needed a bit of time on his own to look for her replacement.

Evelyn huffed out something that was a cross between a laugh and a sigh. What a ridiculous thought. That wasn't likely his intention for sending her alone. She knew Eric loved her. At least most of the time she knew it. It was just that her emotions were such a tumult right now and it was difficult for her to imagine *why* he would love her. But that was ridiculous. Even if he didn't love her anymore, he didn't wish her to be killed in a foreign country. It would be easy enough for her to get killed in her own country.

All right, now she was just being ridiculous. It was time for a change of perspective.

Yes, her husband should have come with her as they had planned. No, he wasn't there as planned. But yes, she was doing just fine. In fact, it could be argued that she was having a great time. She ought to be. The weather was gorgeous, the scenery was too. The pastries were to die for. She had been dreaming of this trip as long as she could remember. There was no reason not to be having a great time. Perhaps she was delusional.

She shook her head. At least she had managed just fine on her own thus far.

Already she had learned to do new things. She had managed all her connections and hadn't gotten lost or even turned around. And now she was in a café alone. It wasn't the worst experience ever. Evelyn was determined to come out the other end of this content and transformed. Because she needed some transforming, that was for certain.

For one thing, she had to accept that they were going to be a family of two forever. The only way she was going to survive not having a baby was by accepting it. She was getting a little too close to forty. In fact, in just a few months she'd be hitting the last year before that dreaded milestone. No babies would be blessing them.

But that was okay, wasn't it? People didn't die from childlessness, did they?

And Eric had finally agreed to take in a foster child. Evelyn had been researching that option for months but it had taken Eric much longer to warm to the idea. When he had agreed to that, she had agreed to stop putting every last cent they had into fertility treatments. And that's where the money for this trip came from. Because they had decided it rather on the spur of the moment, Evelyn had actually been able to find some great last-minute deals. The flights were a sell-off rate. And the tiny little apartment she could barely turn around in had been a steal. Which was why she hadn't canceled everything when Eric said, the day before they were set to leave, that he couldn't get away after all but that she should go on her own.

The delicious croissant turned to sawdust in her mouth at the sudden thought that entered her head.

Was Eric having an affair?

Was that why he didn't want to come with her on what was supposed to be a romantic trip? Evelyn had thought they would be able to find their way back to the close bond they'd shared before she'd become obsessed with motherhood. She had truly hoped this trip would help get them on the right track.

Instead, she was here, in one of the most beautiful places she'd ever seen feeling decidedly wrong-footed. She was even more of an emotional mess than she would have been if he was with her. She couldn't speak the language, she was deeply jetlagged, and she was going to get lost at every turn down the rabbit warren of little streets.

But even the cramped roads had their beauty, she acknowledged to herself as she sipped the tiny coffee that was helping to restore her equilibrium. She should have asked for the coffee to come in a bowl or an entire pot, she thought as she reached the bottom of the cup with a final sip. That was one more thing she was going to have to adjust to. The portion sizes were not what she was used to.

She should have come for even longer. Eating and drinking European portion sizes might help her fit into that dream dress she had bought when she had finally accepted that pregnancy wasn't something she was going to experience for herself.

Evelyn's circuitous and less than helpful thoughts were finally interrupted by a familiar jingle. Someone was video calling. For the space of a heartbeat Eve thought it might be Eric and her delight leapt. But he never used Facetime. Even before she pulled her phone out of her bag, Evelyn knew it had to be one of her friends.

"Tina!" Evelyn exclaimed, more surprised than she ought to be. "What a delight," she said as she swiped into the call

Tina's sarcastic grin filled the small screen. "You didn't think I'd let you keep that gorgeous place all to yourself, did you? I expect you to show me where you are now that I can see for myself that you made it in one piece."

"Didn't you get my text?"

"Do you mean the three words you must have dashed off as you were waiting for your suitcase?" Tina asked with an eyeroll. "That hardly counts."

Evelyn was embarrassed to be talking on a speakerphone in the crowded coffee shop but was too happy to hear from her friend to terminate the conversation. It was so refreshing to be reminded that someone cared about her after she had been feeling so glum moments before.

"I haven't paid my tab yet so I can't show you the views, but check out this cute little café," Evelyn said, turning the camera around so that Tina could see the décor surrounding her.

"It's very you," Tina said with a grin. "But seriously. I can see you made it there physically, but how are you really? Besides the jetlag," she added when Evelyn had opened her mouth to say she was tired.

A laugh huffed out of her. Evelyn could always count on the more acerbic woman to call her on any attempts to fool herself or others.

"I'll be ok, but I'm still a little stunned to find myself here by myself."

Tina nodded. "I can only imagine." Her frown of commiseration filled the screen even as she seemed to be searching Evelyn's features. "Do you think you're going to feel safe there? I know you said you wanted to see it all for yourself even if you had to do it alone. Do you still feel that way now that you're there?"

"I really do, Tina. And when you called, I was just thinking that maybe being alone will be for the best."

"You're too romantic to believe that," Tina scoffed, forcing another laugh from Evelyn's belly.

"I understand why you'd say that, but why I think it might be good is because a total change of scenery will make me reconsider myself."

"Are you thinking of a makeover?"

"Maybe a reckoning."

Tina's grin was full of approval. "That's the spirit."

"I should go, Tina. I need to walk off the massive croissant I just ate."

"Okay, Eve, I need to get on with my day, too, but I just wanted to check in."

"I truly appreciate it, Tina. Give your little guy a squeeze for me."

"Will do. Eat a croissant for me."

Evelyn was laughing even as she clicked the end button. It was a surprise to hear from the other woman. Evelyn had never really considered herself terribly close with the veterinarian. She was more a friend by association. Evelyn had become friends with Rachel, who lived next door to her and Eric. Rachel's aunt Eileen had been Evie's best friend since she and Eric had moved to the island. Rachel had become her friend when she'd inherited her aunt's house after that dear woman's untimely death from cancer. Two of Rachel's old schoolmates had come into Evelyn's circles along with Rachel. But she hadn't necessarily considered them to be really her friends. It was lovely to hear from Tina.

It also highlighted the fact that Eric hadn't called her.

Enough! Evelyn ordered herself firmly as she again turned her attention to the spectacular view before her. Yes, she was in a romantic location by herself. Wasn't the south of France the honeymoon capital of the world? Or was that Paris? Never mind. Nice was a romantic place, no argument. But it was a romantic location because it was beautiful. That didn't have to be the exclusive domain of couples. While she wanted, even longed to reconnect with her husband, she really needed to reconnect with herself.

Who was she? Evelyn, as an individual, not as a wife or as a wishful mother, but as a person, an adult, a middle-aged adult, at that? What had the last thirty-eight years culminated in for Evelyn?

Why not figure it out during her month in Nice? That would be far more productive than wallowing in self-pity or lamenting the fact that Eric had stayed home. She didn't want to make him feel badly about having to work. Well, maybe she did, but she didn't *want* to want it. If she shifted her focus, surely she could show herself a good time and have pleasant things to tell him about so he could feel included in her metamorphosis. Maybe they could find their way back to each other even from a distance, or at least when she went home.

Maybe she had put her expectations too high on a trip anyhow. Thinking it would fix their marriage might have set them up for disappointment. Maybe that was why Eric had found a flimsy excuse to stay home.

That was fine. France would be for her, then. And didn't she deserve it after the monumental loss she had agreed to face?

Feeling resolved and determined to see the positive, Evelyn opened the camera app on her phone and angled it so she could catch her coffee cup, plate, and a view of the sea.

I made it in one piece and found a great café. Was too much in need of the caffeine to take a pic before consuming so all you get are the crumbs - smiley face

She quickly hit the send button with a nod and a smile. That was exactly the right tone. No recriminations or complaints but not too overjoyed either. To her surprise, before she could even put her phone away it pinged with an incoming message.

Chapter Two

Eric McConnell ran a hand through his hair, stared at his phone and the message on its screen, and wondered how to respond. He had barely slept all night worrying about his wife traveling alone and so was still in bed despite it being nearly eight in the morning. Eight in the morning on a work day. When he had told his wife he couldn't go with her due to an emergency at work. With a shake of his head Eric refocused his thoughts onto his wife and his worries about her being so far away on her own.

Evelyn never went anywhere by herself except to run errands or go for a walk within a couple miles of their house, especially not since she'd taken leave from her office job in order to focus exclusively on getting pregnant. Unsuccessfully, he added with a heavy sigh. He probably ought to feel something other than just relief. Obviously, he was glad she had made it all right. But other than that, he was numb to everything else. Numb to their agreed upon loss of children. Numb to the thought of never being a father. Not a real one anyway. Numb to Evelyn's grief. Even numb to the fear that something might happen to her while she was away.

He had called himself all manner of fool for sending her off on her own. He was glad her text confirmed she had made it and didn't seem too angry with him for not being there with her. But those feelings were a little distant. As though he were witnessing them rather than feeling them. He was enshrouded in fog. He did know that he was the biggest fool to walk the earth.

What sort of man needs a break from his wife? He ought to be with her, consoling her, not running from her grief. But he just needed a bit of time to pull himself together. He had thought sending her off to a tourist destination she'd always wanted to see would mean she'd be safe and distracted while he figured himself out. He had his own grief to cope with, he supposed. He couldn't really deal with hers just then.

Eric swung his legs over the side of the bed. He had sort of forgotten about the time zone thing. He hadn't slept well, so it was already eight o'clock in the morning here on the Cape, on this side of the Atlantic, but on her side, he supposed it must be around two o'clock in the afternoon. He glanced around the room. It was still as tidy as she had left it. He couldn't mess it up in one day, especially when most of the time she'd been gone he'd been trying to sleep. With a shake of his head, he turned his attention back to his phone.

Thanks for the msg. Was starting to worry. Love the color of the water.

He should have said "Love you" but they didn't really say that to each other anymore. Not that he didn't feel it. Down to the soles of his feet and everywhere in between, he loved his wife more than life itself. There was no question in his mind about that. He just didn't know how to show her or tell her. He had failed her in so many ways that he didn't even know how to be with her anymore.

Sending her off on that trip was the coward's way; he freely admitted it to himself even as he acknowledged that he was going to grow an ulcer over the next weeks as he worried about his wife on a different continent all by herself.

Was she street-smart enough to be safe? Of course, she wasn't. What if she was hurt in some way? She wouldn't be able to communicate. No one would know to contact him.

He was a fool *and* a coward. He could only hope she found a way to enjoy herself on her own. She had at least managed to order some food. That was good. And she had found her way to her destination.

The heat of embarrassment filled him as another realization struck him. Apparently, she didn't need him as much as he would have liked to think or as much as he'd always thought she did. Yes, she contacted him way later than he had expected her to, but it would seem she had managed her connections and whatever she had to do to get from the airport to that café. She had managed on her own. Without him.

Why had he sent her off on her own?

He had always taken pride in looking after her. Now she was going to figure out that she didn't need him after all. He was an idiot.

But he knew why he had sent her on the trip without him. He just couldn't go with her. They had been right to decide to stop trying to get pregnant. He couldn't live with Evelyn's disappointment month after month when she got her period like clockwork. She had always kept her feelings to herself, for the most part, but you'd have to be a piece of stone or ice not to realize her heart was breaking each and every time.

He wanted to be a father. It was natural, of course. He wanted to be a natural father. A man who got his wife pregnant the normal way. And then nine months later a little critter emerged that looked a little bit like each of its parents. But that wasn't going to happen for them. It wasn't for lack of trying on their part, that was certain.

They had tried the natural way for years. They'd been together most of their adult lives. After they'd gotten married, they'd agreed to let nature take its course. When children blessed them with their presence, they'd do so. So, they hadn't been preventing pregnancy nor actively pursuing it. Not at first anyway.

As time passed and the years went by, though, Evelyn had become increasingly fixated on pregnancy and parenthood. She had changed their diet, their positions, their sleep patterns, everything she could think of or read about that might lend itself toward their getting pregnant.

For several months they'd had sex as often as possible, which turned out not to be as fun as one would think when it was on an agenda. When that hadn't worked, then Evelyn had decreed that they couldn't do it at all except when she was at her peak fertility, hoping that would somehow lend itself to success.

When all those attempts failed, then they'd started seeing doctors. Eric had never been poked or prodded and nearly violated so much in his entire life as he had been in the last three years as they chased after their dreams of parenthood.

Finally, they had agreed it wasn't going to happen. The doctors didn't even seem to have a reasonable explanation as to why they couldn't get pregnant. It seemed Evelyn's uterus was hostile. Such a stupid expression. Nothing about his wife was hostile. But it wouldn't hold onto fertilized eggs. They didn't even consider it miscarriage. Somehow they were just never pregnant.

And he had to live with an inconsolable wife.

They had, of course, considered adoption. But that was such a long and expensive process. It was still Eric's first choice. Or rather his second, after having a birth child. It was the second-best way of being sure you could keep the child. But Evelyn had now become fixated on their becoming foster parents. And after her talking about it for months, Eric had finally agreed. They had been assessed and approved. They had taken courses and classes. Now there was just more waiting. But they had continued to hope and pray for a biological child, despite going through the steps in preparation for fostering.

It wasn't so much that Eric was opposed to the idea, but he didn't think it was going to be any less heartbreaking. Could his already fragile wife handle the tentativeness of fostering? Eric didn't know if *he* could handle the not knowing when or if a child might get pulled from them. He could just picture them falling in love with some kiddo only to have him or her returned to a situation they had no control over. How was his warm-hearted wife supposed to cope with that?

Rather than discussing it or facing it, Eric had signed all the necessary documents to become a foster parent and then he'd sent his wife off on her own to France. And stayed home, in their dream home, on the beach. On the wrong side of the Atlantic. He was a fool.

Chapter Three

Evelyn blinked at the screen of her phone, needing to adjust the brightness in order to see it in the early afternoon sunlight streaming in through the café's large windows. Eric's response had been quicker than she'd expected. She'd thought she'd already be out on the promenade by the time he got back to her. Instead, she was still in the bustle of the small café. She ought to vacate her spot, but she felt like a cat who didn't want to leave her sunny spot.

He had been worried? Well then why hadn't he messaged her? Even Tina had called. Why hadn't he come with her if he was going to go and worry about her? Once more a combination of anger and despair welled up within her only to be sent back from where it came. Such emotions certainly weren't going to help her right now.

But why had he worried about her? Evelyn cut the unhelpful thoughts off. She was glad, in a certain way, that he had worried about her. That supported the thought that he at least still cared to a certain extent. Surely, she could work with that.

And he "loved the colors." Of course, he did. How could he not? They were even better in real life. But she wouldn't point that out to him. He would certainly be able to figure that out for himself. He wasn't an idiot.

Glancing around the small café again made Evie a little uncomfortable. She shouldn't stay there too much longer or she would feel obligated to order something else. Every spot was filled. The small business would probably rather serve someone else rather than have her occupying a spot. And really, despite how small the coffee had been, she ought to go for a walk and try to orient herself rather than ordering another.

If she could manage to stay awake a few more hours, it would go a long way to reducing the length of time she struggled with jetlag. It was one more of the things she had researched when planning the trip. Jetlag was a real concern, especially for middle-aged Americans arriving in Europe. But she'd learned that if she stayed up as long as she could, hydrated, especially with vitamin water, she'd be much better off. She had planned accordingly. She suited her thought to actions and pulled a bottle of electrolyte water from her bag, keeping her gaze fixed out the window.

And it might take her the entire month of her stay to grow immune to seeing the Middle Ages architecture and the clay roofs, the blue on blue of the cloudless sky where it met the turquoise of the Baie des Anges, the cliffs and the rocks. Everything she'd been dreaming of seeing since she was a girl. Or maybe it would never happen. But she was going to make a valiant effort at it by gazing at it every waking moment of her time there. Not that it mattered if she never grew immune. Gorgeous was gorgeous and ought to be admired.

Not all water was created equal. Was it disloyal to her own backyard ocean to love the Mediterranean so much? She hoped not. She truly loved the home she and Eric had made on Cape Avalon. The decade they'd been living in their beautiful home had been the most content she'd been in her entire life despite the fertility struggles they'd been dealing with in the last few years. The ocean in their backyard was one of the things she loved most about it.

The Mediterranean was a different sort of gorgeous from the beauty of the Atlantic that surrounded their island home. Cape Avalon was the most beautiful place she had ever been and she loyally asserted that it still was. But this might be as beautiful. Just a different beautiful. Evelyn shook her head. Maybe she was too tired to make sense. But no one had to know. She didn't have to speak to another person for a whole month if she didn't want to.

Not that she would really be able to even if she wanted to, she thought rather nervously as she glanced back at her phone. She would have to make sure she always kept the thing charged up. She was going to need her translation app frequently.

She hadn't yet gotten very far with her language learning app. She'd always meant to learn French, considering it a beautiful language since she had heard it a few times growing up. But she had been preoccupied with other things and had only given a half-hearted effort to the hobby. Her parents had thought trying to learn languages was pretentious. Evelyn didn't want to think about that right now. Now would be the perfect time to pursue her new hobby. She pinned a bright smile to her face and raised her arm.

"L'addition, s'il vous plait."

She must have said it right. Within moments the waiter had brought her the bill, she'd paid, and then found herself on her way again. So far, she hadn't found anyone to be as standoffish as the internet had led her to believe the people would be in Nice. That was a relief. Despite her determination to concentrate on her own self-improvement over the following weeks, Evelyn didn't think she'd be able to actually go an entire month without interacting with others around her.

Leaving the little coffee shop—*patisserie*, she repeated to herself—Evelyn tried to make a mental note of where exactly she was in relation to where she had started. She wanted to walk along the promenade and absorb a little more sunshine and enjoy the view before going back to her apartment. It was much too early in the day for her to go to bed now despite the night of no sleep. If she went and had a nap, she wouldn't sleep that night and then she'd have a serious problem with jetlag for days.

Walking was on the agenda, then. That and looking for opportunities to practice her French. It was the first time in her life that she had so little she had to do. Nothing really. How truly decadent. Her parents would likely think that too was pretentious. But she was going to bask in it while it lasted. It was likely only to be the length of her trip. When she returned home, she would have to resume being gainfully employed. And there was also the hoped-for-child to think about. For now, she would enjoy the lovely nothingness.

But her worry-wart brain needed a to-do list, so she started to think through what she wished to accomplish during her month alone. She had been too nervous and borderline furious on the plane to think about it, but she needed to make a plan. The whole point of this trip was that she was supposed to be getting over her grief at finally accepting they wouldn't be parents. That was supposed to lead them back to the close relationship they had once enjoyed. She didn't want that to be completely overshadowed by being angry with Eric. A plan was definitely called for.

For one thing, she had no intention of returning to the job she had taken a sabbatical from when she and Eric had agreed to give child-bearing one more emphatic try. The doctor had suggested that it was stress interfering with her ability to conceive. For that reason she had taken a leave of absence from her job. She had always thought she liked her work, but the extent of her relief over not going in to the office where she was the assistant to three very busy executives every day indicated to her that she had, in fact, only liked the routine. Keeping up with all the minute details of keeping the schedules for three vice presidents of a very large corporation was not something she wished to revisit.

If they were going to foster a child, she wanted to be home for that child. So she would have to come up with a source of income she could generate without leaving the house. Not to say that they really needed the money, especially if they would no longer be paying fertility doctors. But kids were expensive, or so she'd read. Again with the sarcasm.

Evelyn gave her head a shake as she turned it up to face the sun. It was much warmer in April in Nice than it was on the Cape. She appreciated the heat on her face. Hopefully it would melt away her restive thoughts.

She strolled along the promenade, which was more crowded than she would have expected on a weekday morning. Apparently, she wasn't the only one on vacation, hoping to avoid the more crowded summertime rush. The fatigue from the long night of travel was pulling at her and part of her longed to either slump into one of the blue chairs along the edge of the concrete wharf or return to her apartment to sleep. But the walk would do her good after all the sitting at an altitude. She tried not to be paranoid, but she knew a long flight like that carried the possibility of blood clots. And as they had already determined with her fertility, she wasn't getting any younger. Clots were actually a risk. A good walk would help mitigate those risks.

If she was going to be partaking of extra-large croissants like the one she'd just enjoyed on a regular basis during her stay, lots of walking was definitely called for anyway. She would keep going. The promenade was a novelty she would enjoy, to be sure. Walking on the elevated concrete extra wide sidewalk was such a treat. It afforded an exceptional view of the bay and the sea beyond.

It would be no hardship to stare at the waves, that was certain. It was one of her favorite things to do at the beach, any beach. The sound here intrigued her. She supposed it was because the waves were crashing onto rocks and pebbles rather than the sand she was used to on Avalon.

Despite her determination to keep her thoughts positive, she couldn't help their turn toward Eric and her mixed up feelings about his text message.

Why had he worried? Did he regret not coming with her? She hoped so. Not that she really wished negative thoughts or feelings on him. She really did love him despite the distance they had allowed to grow between them.

Evelyn stopped and stared out toward the horizon. How could she minimize that distance even, well, from this distance? She sighed. She would have to try hard to share the experience with him. It could even be fun. It would give her something to do, something to work toward. She had just given up her greatest project. She definitely needed a new one.

Of course, she hoped for another project, just an altered one. She might not be going to give birth, but she really hoped there would still be children in their future. She and Eric would be in a much better position to help the poor children who'd be coming into their lives if they were in a good place in their marriage. The distance that had grown between them wasn't welcome. It had crept in unnoticed. But she saw it now. She had hoped to discuss it face to face with Eric, here on their romantic vacation, but maybe she could just eliminate it.

She only hoped sharing her trip from a distance didn't have the opposite effect. That would rot. She would just have to ask him. Ignoring concerns hadn't gotten them anywhere good. That was the whole reason they were where they were. Ignorance was not always bliss.

She would share first, ask later.

With that thought in mind, she snapped a couple pictures of the view and even took a selfie, then quickly sent them to Eric with a short note. *Pic doesn't quite show the color but that blue!!* She thought to add "miss you" on the end but deleted it before sending. That wasn't the note she wanted to convey even if it was true. No recriminations.

She ought to check in with her friends too. A quick, breezy text would suffice. She had already talked with Tina but Rachel and Angela would surely wonder what had become of her. If they weren't all tied up in their own lives each of them had assured her they would have come with her. But Tina had a son who was too young to be left on his own and too busy to leave for very long with his grandparents, and Rachel was still a newlywed who couldn't fathom leaving her husband for a pleasure trip. Angela's family probably could have managed without her but Evelyn wasn't very close with her, she was more a friend of a friend.

"Maybe we'll surprise you for a few days in the middle," Rachel had said earnestly.

"It's only a month," Evelyn had replied. "I'm sure I'll find plenty to do to keep me occupied, don't worry about me. I had actually worried it wasn't long enough when it was going to be two of us. But I think it'll be just right for just me."

Her friends had squeezed her tight, obviously trying to be positive about it, but Evelyn could see they were worried about what it all meant.

Evelyn sighed and shook her hair out of her face. She wasn't doing that great at positivity, was she? She asked herself with a tight laugh as she took a deep breath of the fresh sea air. It wasn't very salty. As someone who hadn't grown up near salt water, she never failed to be surprised that it didn't smell overly salty. Even at home, despite the clear evidence that the air was, in fact, salty, it didn't really smell that way. She wasn't sure why she had thought the Mediterranean might be different from the Atlantic, it really was just a different part of the same body of water.

Her phone jingled, indicating the arrival of a text message. Several, in fact, she could see when she dug her phone out of her back pocket.

Looking good! Have a blast! – Rachel

Hot stuff! – Angela

Evelyn had to laugh over her friends' overuse of exclamation marks. They might be trying just a little too hard, but she loved them for it anyway.

Thanks for sharing, babe. – Eric

Evie grinned. Relief tingled in her fingers. She had struck the right tone with her husband. She would try to continue the trend. She would try to focus on one of Rachel's favorite sayings: Life is full of choices. Choose wisely.

Somehow, she found that inspirational rather than oppressive or fear-inspiring. She was determined to make better choices going forward.

She just needed to figure out what those were.

That was what her focus was going to be during these four weeks in France. First up, how far did she want to walk? Angela's husband was a sports player of some sort and Angela was really fit, she would probably have some good advice.

If you had this view to walk beside, how far would you go? E.

It was probably silly to be asking for such advice but it felt good to include her friends on this journey.

Until my toenails fell off!! – Angela

Winky face

With a huff of light laughter and a shrug of her shoulders, Evelyn assured herself she might not want to walk that far, but surely she hadn't yet walked far enough. She would try to walk the entire length of the promenade and back, getting a good overview of what there was to see along this most touristy part of the city. Then she'd find a proper meal to eat before she allowed herself to crash into bed.

The beach was gorgeous but not varied. Unlike the beach at home. It would probably have its moods like any sea, but the beach in the Baie des Anges felt very groomed – no footsteps could be seen in the pebbles, there was no seaweed, and Evelyn couldn't spot a single bit of litter. It clearly was well taken care of, she realized with a laugh as she spotted a yellow bulldozer parked up against the concrete wall that separated the beach from the promenade. Obviously they plowed the pebbles back into place if they were ever so disobedient as to move from their designated spot. How strange.

Being by herself gave her more opportunity for people watching than if she was with a friend or her husband, and maybe she needed that. She tried not to stare but everything was so interesting. Was that because she was so unused to doing anything by herself or was it a product of being so tired? Or maybe the French were just that much more interesting than the people she was usually around.

Maybe not more interesting, just different, she told herself with a smug smile as she continued walking, watching a group of older men deeply engrossed in an animated conversation from the corner of her eye. A couple of the men were in the blue chairs lined up all along the promenade, the others were standing about gesticulating as if to emphasize whatever point they were making. The ends of their slowly burning cigarettes seemed to only punctuate the conversation while the edges of their mustaches appeared to quiver with the emotion behind what was being said. She wished she could understand the language enough to have a clue what they were discussing. Whatever it was, all of them seemed completely involved, not a single one was checking his phone or looking around for something more interesting.

This was what she needed to learn—to be more engrossed in the here and now. Evelyn couldn't remember the last conversation she'd had with anyone that didn't involve cellphones being consulted at various points. She and Eric were the worst at that. Eric, especially, but that was usually work related. Evie supposed the people whose money he managed felt they had the right to contact him whenever they felt inclined. But that was no excuse, she told herself firmly. That would have to go on her list of things to improve when she went home. Maybe Eric would agree to a phone-free period each evening, especially over dinner or something. That would be particularly important when they finally had a child in their lives. He or she would need their undivided attention.

Okay, Evie, how do you stay engrossed in the moment?

She almost shrugged at the question in her mind and looked around sheepishly hoping no one thought she was an idiot. She then chastised herself for the insecure thought. No one here knew her from a hole in the ground. What did it matter what anyone thought of her? And she kind of was an idiot, so they'd at least be accurate.

Okay, back to the matter at hand. How to stay engrossed. She supposed engaging her senses was important. Evelyn took a deep breath and closed her eyes for a moment. The air smelled of fresh lemons, salty seawater, and what was that? Cinnamon? Yes, that must be from the *boulangerie* across the street. Good. What about her other senses? Sense of hearing? She closed her eyes and listened. The steady sound of the sea rolling the rocks around gave a continuous hum, like white noise, and pedestrians walking and talking all around her added to the effect. It was soothing and rhythmic. Evelyn rubbed her fingers together while she turned her face, still with her eyes closed, more firmly straight on to the sun. The air was dry despite being right next to the sea and the warmth came in waves as the wind moved it around, the sun was hot, not to the point of discomfort, but she was glad she had used her moisturizer that contained a high SPF. Taste? Did she taste anything? She could still taste that coffee she'd enjoyed at the café. The air had smelled fresh but she supposed it also tasted fresh. Could you taste the air? Yes, she could, she asserted to herself.

Evelyn opened her eyes to engage her sense of sight. There was so much to see. She, of course, had already turned her face away from the sun, not having any desire to burn her retinas. But it was still very bright in the afternoon light. The blue of the cloudless sky and the very different but even more beautiful blue of the gently churning sea were amazing. Blue was too bland a word for these gorgeous views. What would one call it? Azure? Turquoise? Aquamarine? The hues kept changing with the light and the angles. And then they were also reflected in some of the buildings. Once she started going to art galleries, she would probably see the same colors reflected there. She didn't think she would ever get tired of looking at it. Evelyn knew she would be spending a lot of time at the beach during her month here.

Stay in the moment. This *moment*, she reminded herself, *not the next one, not next week.*

Right now, how do you feel?

Tired. Evelyn grinned. She was so tired. *But beneath that, I suppose I'm a mixture of bewildered about how I ended up across the world all by myself. But I'm also excited to see what the month holds, not to get out of the moment, but it's going to be an exciting experience, I'm sure of it.*

Evelyn opened her eyes that she hadn't even realized she had closed again and grinned. She was determined to get better in touch with her own thoughts and feelings.

That was how she was going to use this month to her advantage. She was going to grow as a person by figuring out who she, Evelyn, really was.

Evelyn sighed. Was she going to have to figure out where she came from to figure out who she was? Most likely. *Why does everything have to stem from your childhood?*

Thinking about her childhood rarely brought her good feelings. It wasn't so much that she had been mistreated. Except ignoring your children was a form of mistreatment, so she supposed she had been. Discomfort squirmed in her belly. She hated to think back to that time. She hadn't seen anyone in her family in so long. She had chosen to make her own family with friends and neighbors. And Eric. And that was the crux of the matter, wasn't it? Did she still have Eric? He was really all that mattered to her. Why had she made having a baby such a focus for so long? What if she had pushed him away and she was no longer as important to him as he was to her? What if her desire to supplant her crappy childhood by making a baby had made him rethink his priorities toward her?

Evelyn thought about their goodbye at the airport. It had felt rather stilted. She had never truly said goodbye to her husband before. She remembered the passionate farewells from early in their marriage when they had just been parting for the day. Now, she would be away from her husband for a month and she only felt slightly nervous about whether or not she had left enough food in the freezer for him and if she would be able to manage her connections on her own.

She knew for certain that she loved her husband. True, the passage of time might have worn away a little of the heat, but she truly, deeply, even madly loved him. But she supposed she was still angry with him for sending her off without him. What kind of man would do that if he didn't want something bad to happen to his wife? Melodramatic much? Evie asked herself with a roll of her eyes.

Saying goodbye at the airport had been awkward as all get out. Evelyn had so many thoughts and feelings she was keeping to herself for fear of the blowup that would result. There hadn't been time. Between her final packing and trying to leave the house ready for him, she hadn't been able to really tell him how she felt about his decision. It was likely there was much he was keeping to himself, too. Like why on earth he was doing it.

But at the airport wasn't the time to figure it out.

"Take care of yourself," she had said. Even with the passage of time, Evelyn still cringed at how weak and ineffective that had sounded. She should have thrown her arms around his neck and kissed him in such a way that even if he weren't already regretting letting her go, he would then. But she had barely pressed her dry lips to his cheek before she'd said something scattered about getting through security and waved as she hurried away. He might have said something to her, she didn't know as there was too much noise in the huge open space filled with other passengers hurrying by. She'd barely turned to wave once more as she'd joined the line-up for the security scan.

She needed to tell him she was sorry about that. Maybe right after she made peace with herself.

With a shake of her head, Evelyn set off again, quickening her pace in an effort to outrun her thoughts. Her legs weren't capable of that sort of speed, she reminded herself with a wry, silent chuckle. Perhaps she was going to completely lose her mind while she was alone in Nice.

Okay, Evie, she consoled herself, bringing her pace back to a normal stroll. That was a good start. Sixty seconds was the extent of her ability to remain in the moment for a first try. A literal moment to stay in the moment. It didn't matter. She had time. And she now understood that it was going to be important.

Too bad she hadn't brought a shrink with her on the vacation.

Evelyn thought about the books her friends had recommended to her. Rachel's list of reading material had included a book that seemed to lend itself toward psychology. Perhaps she would read a little of that every day. This would be a journey of self-improvement, then.

Casting her gaze beyond the immediate confines of the city, all Evelyn could see were tree-covered hills. There were obviously some communities up there because she could just make out the clay tiled roofs hidden amongst the leaves. Curiosity filled her as to what they would look like. She was apparently going to get herself into shape both physically and mentally while she was on her vacation. Eric would hardly recognize her when she got home. And that might just be a great thing.

Life was full of choices. Evelyn was determined to choose wisely.

She would choose happiness. Whatever she decided that looked like. She would choose a family. Even if that family ended up only being her and Eric and their friends. If it turned out that they really couldn't have their own children, whether adopted or fostered, then they would be the very best honorary auntie and uncle their friends' children could have. And she was going to get back to that confident and passionate woman she had once believed herself to be. For that she needed Eric's cooperation, or maybe it was support she needed. Whatever the case, she was going to give it a true effort. But if he had already checked out, then she was going to figure out how to be the best Evelyn she could be.

One step at a time. That was all it was going to take. As soon as she figured out what the steps were.

Chapter Four

Eric could barely look at his phone after Evelyn's latest text.

Love you lots had been the only message attached to another sea picture.

Why was she sending him pictures? Was she trying to chastise him for sending her off on her own? Or was that just his own guilty conscience smiting him? Of course it was just his guilt talking. His sweet Evie would never be so passive aggressive. She probably just felt badly for his missing out on the beautiful views. He ought to be grateful, not irritated.

He thought about turning off his notifications. But his wife was on the other side of the ocean in a different time zone, different language, very different setting. The least he could do to show even a crumb of support for her was to leave his notifications on and respond whenever she messaged him. She was probably lonely. And nervous. Maybe even scared.

How could he have sent her off on her own?

Eric laced up his sneakers and let himself out of the house to go for a jog. If he stayed home any longer, he was likely to kick a hole in the walls.

He stepped out the back door and took in a deep breath of fresh air as he stared at the beautiful blue of his own sky. It wasn't quite the same as where she was, but it would have to do. And do quite nicely, in fact. At least it wasn't overcast.

Somehow that thought propelled him down the steps off his back porch and on to the sandy path leading to the beach. Despite telling his wife there was a work emergency preventing him from going with her on the dream vacation, he wasn't really all that busy. There was no need to be at his office until noon at the earliest. He didn't even have to go at all, if he didn't want to. He'd taken to using work as an escape. With the house to himself, he was looking forward to enjoying their beautiful home that backed up to the Atlantic.

Guilt gnawed at him with that thought. He shouldn't be so happy his wife wasn't home. And in some ways, he wasn't. He loved her and was absolutely certain he would miss her. But since he constantly felt as though he was letting her down, the fact that she wasn't there was a bit of a relief. That was his problem, though, not her fault. Maybe he'd be able to figure out how to get over that while she was away.

Or maybe they should go to therapy. Not maybe; they definitely needed to seriously consider it.

It really couldn't be healthy that he was both disappointed and deeply relieved that she had agreed to go on that trip without him. He never should have given her the option. He should be walking on that stupid concrete sidewalk with her. What had she called it? A promenade, whatever that was. She seemed to think it was spectacular. And of course, from her pictures, it was. But he just couldn't deal with her grief over their infertility.

It had been such a relief to him that she had agreed to stop treatments that he felt like the worst sort of louse to ever exist. What sort of man was he that he hadn't wanted to do everything humanly possible to get his wife pregnant?

Don't get him wrong, he enjoyed certain aspects of it. He couldn't even muster a grin over that thought, though, as his feet pounded the hardened sand beneath his sneakers and sweat started to creep down his neck. How had it become a chore? Trying to have a baby should have drawn him and Evelyn together. Instead, it had brought silence and sadness into their marriage.

It was his fault.

Not the infertility, apparently. The doctors still didn't have a solid answer as to why they had never conceived. According to all the tests, they should have been able to do so. While they weren't in perfect, twenty-year-old shape, there was nothing definitive to point to. But despite the medicine, the shots, the affirmations and meditations, everything short of voodoo that Evelyn had been willing to try, they couldn't get pregnant.

At least they had never actually lost a pregnancy. Eric didn't think his soft-hearted wife would have been able to survive that sort of loss. Losing out on the potential had been blow enough. Month after month of getting her cycle right on time had become something to mourn for her, not just the regular moods that a woman went through when she got her period. His Evelyn would actually go into mourning. He just couldn't take it anymore.

She hadn't ever been loud about it. But then the silences were actually worse, in his mind. If she had wept and wailed and then moved along, he could have comforted her and then perhaps gotten over it. Instead, he had been left to feel useless—a man's least favorite feeling in existence.

And the thought of watching her quietly mourn while it should have been a romantic adventure had just made him ill. That was why he couldn't go with her. But that had been the coward's way. He knew that, but he hadn't been able to go through with the trip. And he hadn't bothered to explain himself.

He didn't know what was going to happen to Evelyn if their neighbor got pregnant. Since Rachel and Jake got married, he dreaded that announcement whenever he saw them. That was why he avoided them like they carried a plague. He knew even Evelyn too, had started spending less time with her friend.

Isolation couldn't possibly be good for her. And now she was completely isolated on the other side of this vast body of water. He shook his head even as sweat began to drip into his eyes. His lungs were starting to burn. But no matter how fast he ran, he couldn't outrun his thoughts.

He ought to be with his wife. He had failed her even in this. He should still go. Surprise her. Turn up in France and go ahead with their romantic trip of a lifetime. But as much as he loved her and wished he could do it, he just couldn't make himself go.

Digging deep into reserves of energy that didn't exist, Eric put even more effort into his run, barely acknowledging the neighbors he passed or encountered. It might be a futile attempt but he was going to do his best to outrun his disquiet.

Chapter Five

Evelyn had walked until the soles of her feet were sore. Despite wearing her most comfortable shoes for the long night of travel, still they were starting to chafe. But she was smiling. She had walked for miles. Almost to the airport! She hadn't meant to walk quite that far, but her thoughts had been chasing her and she had hoped to avoid them by staying in the moment.

She had stayed in the moment all the way to the end of the promenade. Or rather she had returned again and again to the moment, she reminded herself with a grin over her tendency to worry and dwell on the future. It had been challenging until her feet started hurting. Then she didn't want to stay in the moment any longer, or rather not in a negative frame of mind.

Staying in the moment was great until it turned into wallowing. Evelyn started analyzing where the line might fall. For her, right now, she knew thinking about her sore feet wasn't a real issue. Once she got some food into her and then returned to her apartment and had a good sleep, her feet would be fine by morning. So even if it consumed her thoughts now, that wasn't really wallowing.

But if she allowed her grief over their decision to stop trying for a baby or even her concerns over Eric not coming on the trip to overshadow her actual trip, *that* would be wallowing. Evelyn did believe she ought to give those matters serious thought, though, while she was in Nice. The distance might actually give her some perspective on the matter. Or at least better perspective than she'd had at home.

She would have all the privacy she could wish for even while being in a crowd. No one knew her. No one would judge her. Or if they did, it wouldn't have to bother Evelyn in the least since she would never see anyone here ever again.

Walking to the end of the promenade had seemed like a great idea when she had come up with it, but now Evelyn was seriously reconsidering the wisdom of her choice. She heaved a huge sigh of relief when she was about two thirds of the way back to the old part of the city and thus her apartment when she saw a quaint little restaurant that immediately appealed to her.

Evelyn couldn't even explain exactly why it appealed. Maybe she had just reached her limit and needed to rest her feet and feed her exhaustion. But it wasn't too busy. There were tiny little tables with chairs set facing the sea. Yes, it was across a busy street from the sea, but she wasn't going to allow that to mar her enjoyment. They had an English menu and the descriptions sounded both familiar and comforting. Sandwiches with fries, oysters, onion soup, hamburgers, pasta or salad. Perhaps she ought to have "French" onion soup while in France. At this moment, she didn't give the least care to calories. She needed food that would warm her soul.

Of course, if anything was too greasy or heavy, she wouldn't be able to sleep. That was going to be enough of a problem with the time zones, she didn't need to add to the risk with anything too cheesy. She had read that the pizzas in Nice were amazing; she would try and see for herself.

It was a pleasure for her to sit and just enjoy the warm sun with her feet stretched out in front of her. Since she was a short woman, Evelyn didn't have to be overly concerned that she might trip any of the passersby on the sidewalk in front of the little restaurant. Was it because her soul felt cold that she was obsessing over the sunshine? Evelyn dismissed the question quickly.

But wow was she beat. Evelyn suspected she wouldn't have any trouble falling asleep when she finally put her head on a pillow. She was nearly falling asleep right there at her table. Not really. She was still too excited about being there. She had been dreaming of a trip to France for years. Her dream hadn't been to go alone, but that was fine. She was fine. Everything was going to be just fine.

She had contacted their social worker before her flight to let her know they wouldn't be available to take a foster child for at least five or six weeks. Evelyn was glad she had told her well before finding out that Eric wasn't going on the trip with her. There was no need to give them reason to suspect there was any sort of trouble in their marriage. Because there wasn't. Eric and Evelyn had been a strong, solid couple for going on twenty years. Ever since they met in college.

Eric had been everything her younger self had wished for – smart, kind, and so very handsome as a young man, but he had actually improved with age. Like Sean Connery or some other actor who was even more swoony now than when he was young. Swoony. What a great word. It still applied to Eric, that was certain. Even more now than ever. Swoony in all ways, not just in his looks. She thought he was even smarter and kinder than he had been in college. Patient and understanding. Or so she thought.

Except that Evelyn hadn't been doing any swooning of late. She certainly hadn't been telling him how swoon-worthy she found him. And he wasn't a mind reader, so how was he supposed to know?

She hadn't even told him she loved him at the airport. Despite her anger, surely she had felt it and ought to have said it. At least she had said it in text messages since. She really needed to let go of the anger. It wasn't helping anything. Being angry about their infertility wasn't going to help and being angry that Eric wasn't with her wasn't going to make that go away either.

Maybe she ought to talk to Tina about it. Her friend had been a very angry woman until she'd had a bit of a health scare and suddenly turned her whole life around.

Evelyn: How'd you let go of the anger?

Evelyn hadn't meant to actually hit send on that message, but suddenly her phone pinged with a reply and heat flooded her face with embarrassment. Eve rolled her eyes. No one here knew her nor what she had done. There was nothing to be embarrassed about. Except Tina knew what she had done.

Tina: LOL. Good morning to U 2.

Tina: UR awful deep for such a gorgeous place.

There was no arguing with that statement. What could Evelyn text in reply?

Tina: There's no secret sauce. I just let it go.

Tina: Repeatedly LOL

Tina: Not sure if U R referring to Eric or babies, but if U need to talk, call me.

Evelyn snorted with a bit of a laugh. She wasn't yet ready to bleed out all her feelings to her friend, but she appreciated the offer.

Evelyn: Thanks! I'll take you up on it, but not today. Too tired from walking off the jetlag.

Tina: Does that work?

Evelyn: LOL I'll let you know tomorrow

Evelyn shook her head. She had really allowed so many important things to go by the wayside in her frantic effort to become a mother. She hadn't even maintained any friendships, never mind the most important relationship she could have – her husband. Her much-loved husband. She really needed to tell him more.

But motherhood was important, so she refused to beat herself up too much over it. Now that she realized what she had been doing, Evie was determined to do better, but she wouldn't rake herself over the coals for her lapses of judgment of the past. Starting now. Because she had certainly done plenty of that in the past.

Tina's advice was sound. She would let it go. Repeatedly if need be.

It wasn't as though Eric had been falling over himself to tell her he thought she was anything special. Not that it was an excuse. While turnabout might be fair play, Evelyn didn't believe it was any sort of foundation for a happy marriage. While Evie was determined to learn from her mistakes, she wasn't going to wallow in them. If she was going to let it go, she needed to stick with the moment and just do it. Especially here in the most gorgeous of all her dream destinations.

Her thoughts were interrupted by the waitress arriving with her order.

"*Merci*," Evelyn practiced with a smile.

"Will you want anything else?"

Evelyn laughed. It would seem the wait staff were more used to English-speaking tourists than she was used to speaking French. When she shook her head, the waitress nodded and hurried off to serve someone else on the busy patio, allowing Evelyn to return to her thoughts.

She only had a month to enjoy the beautiful south of France. She had no intention of wasting that time with recriminations and regrets. While she ate her pizza, which was delicious but not at all what she was used to, Evelyn made a mental note of what she hoped to see and do the next day while also examining the food in front of her.

The pizza was different from anything she'd had before. The circumference was much larger than she would ever be able to eat on her own. But it was the thinnest crust she had ever seen. And it wasn't crispy, except at the edges where you could hold onto your slice. It really was delicious, but it definitely wouldn't be replacing her favorite pizza place at home. Nothing beat the cheesy pepperoni with an extra thick cheese stuffed crust from Jimmy's Pizza—not even this special Niçoise pizza, it seemed. But maybe she would be willing to try different toppings the next time she and Eric ordered.

Despite the thinness of the crust and her miles of walking, there was no way she was going to be able to eat the whole thing on her own. She lifted a hand in the air. "*L'addition, s'il vous plait. Et une boîte à emporter?*"

Her young waitress gave her a toothy grin and nodded. "*Oui m'dame. Un moment.*"

She smiled. She'd practiced asking for a takeout box on the plane. Looked like her work had paid off.

The waitress disappeared into the restaurant, weaving her way through tables covered in white and red checked tablecloths and topped with pink carnations to a computer by the old wooden bar at the back, returning a moment later with her check and the box. Of course, the wait staff's English was better than her French but she didn't care. She was determined to enjoy her own efforts. She was soon on her way for the last bit of walking before she returned to her small apartment.

Chapter Six

The next day, after a deep, dreamless sleep, Evelyn was congratulating herself on choosing to do all that walking the day before, despite the slight ache in her feet and calves that morning. She was convinced it was why she had been able to sleep so well. With jetlag and being alone in a foreign country, Evelyn had feared she wouldn't sleep despite her fatigue, so she was intensely relieved when she woke up to a bright blue sky after what felt like having just put her head on the pillow. She had no recollection of the night passing, and felt like she'd barely even rolled over.

Perhaps the lack of movement in the night was why she was so very stiff. Never mind all the walking the day before. But that was nothing a bit more walking wouldn't fix.

In her delight in arriving safely in the beautiful city, Evelyn had forgotten that she ought to buy some groceries, so she would have to content herself with what the Niçoise considered breakfast before she ventured out to buy some supplies. Thankfully there was a small bakery two doors down from the quaint little gem of an apartment building Eve was staying in. Her unit was cozy, to say the least, but it felt like an intimate haven from the bustle of the charming neighborhood.

The façade of the buildings blended together almost seeming to be one. The seamless, intricate architectural details intrigued her as she left one door and entered the other.

Evelyn loved the pastries and coffee that passed for *petit dejeuner* in the south of France, but to her, that was what one ate for a snack or coffee break, not the most important meal of the day. With a smile, she looked around at all the happy people bustling around where she sat at a small table in front of the *patisserie*. It wouldn't seem anyone was being harmed by the unusual dietary customs. Perhaps she would have to expand her mind on more than just avenues to motherhood. Apparently eggs and toast weren't the only thing one could eat for breakfast

This brought her attention to what else she could see around her. Everywhere she looked there were mothers and children. Or small families, both moms and dads taking their little ones with them as they ran their errands.

She hadn't been expecting that. Evelyn had thought it would be mostly fellow tourists she would encounter in the highly popular travel destination. How short-sighted to forget that people actually lived in the beautiful city. And if all the apartments were as small as the one she had rented, it was likely no one spent much time at home. She would have to brace herself to encounter the sight throughout her month.

Evelyn's heart sank at the realization while she couldn't help watching one adorable little girl help her mother pick out which fruits they ought to buy at the market. Maybe she would have to buy her own groceries somewhere else. Evie didn't think she could bear the experience. But she was unlikely to be able to avoid seeing families, and would she even want to, she demanded of herself.

A sick feeling continued to churn in her stomach as she stayed in her seat with her coffee held close to her mouth so the slight trembling wouldn't be visible. Her gaze was riveted to the little girl. Evelyn's mind tumbled with possibilities. How would her life be different if she and Eric had been able to get pregnant years ago?

She could have teenagers now, she thought with a widening gaze as she contemplated that possibility, finally able to shift her gaze away from the small child who was still chattering to her mother animatedly. Obviously, Evie couldn't really hear them, nor was she likely to be able to understand their words, but their bond was clear to anyone watching.

Not that Evelyn wanted to be caught watching. Getting arrested for stalking a child while in a foreign country was not her idea of an adventure, she reminded herself with a tremulous smile as she turned her attention to a group of teenagers practicing with skateboards on the steps of what she thought might be a courthouse to her left.

The police didn't appear to be appreciative of the kids' skills and chased them away. It surprised her how powerful the police seemed to be in that city. They were well-armed and roved around in packs. And the teens seemed to have a healthy respect, or at least fear, of the consequences of crossing them. Evie was pretty sure American kids would be sassing back to the cops if they were asked to leave somewhere. Not these teens, despite looking exactly the same as any she would see at home. Evelyn couldn't decide if that was a good thing or not. But she was happy not to witness a confrontation. She didn't think her heart could handle it that day.

She had awoken feeling positive and motivated but somehow, now, after such a seemingly little thing of watching a family, she felt small and deflated once more.

But that wasn't going to be allowed to remain, Evelyn thought with determination as she took the last sip of her cooling coffee. She was here to explore, and explore she would. Let it go, she sternly told herself. Tina's advice applied to both her anger and her despondency.

After quickly settling her bill, and knowing she was likely to be hungry again soon with how unsubstantial her breakfast had been, Evie decided her first order of business was to get some supplies. Since the market in the old city was on her list of things to explore, that was where she would start. It was likely her supplies would be a little more expensive if she bought them at the popular destination, but everything looked so fresh and good, it would be worth it.

Exploring the various stalls was an excellent diversion and soon Evelyn was loaded with more fruit and vegetables and eggs than she was likely to be able to eat before they went bad, but she had enjoyed practicing her beginners' French on the friendly sellers. With a contented sigh, Evelyn finally concluded that she had bought more than enough food for the time being. She would have to stop at a butcher shop at some point if she wanted to have some meat and, of course, the requisite fresh baguette, but for now she had enough. She would drop everything back to her apartment before she set out to explore once more.

Evelyn was determined to become familiar with the streets right around her apartment and maybe climb up the chateau hill that day. It wouldn't be nearly as far a walk as she had accomplished yesterday, but it would still be more than she was used to doing at home, where getting around by car was far more popular than it seemed to be in this pedestrian city.

Walking was making her feel good, though, so she certainly wasn't complaining. It was probably endorphins, but she didn't care what was helping lift her dull mood as long as it was lifted. She couldn't slip into a depression every time she saw a small child. That was no way to live. Besides, she was going to be positive about the foster experience. And maybe she and Eric would be able to keep one or more of the children they would welcome into their home. Fostering was supposed to be temporary, but she had heard several stories of families who were able to make the arrangements more permanent after a while.

Being a mother didn't have to equate with babies. She could and would mother whichever children come into their lives. That didn't make her inadequate as a person. Just because her womb didn't produce those children, that wouldn't mean they were any less hers.

Perhaps if she told herself that often enough, she would believe it.

Just birthing someone didn't make you a good parent to them, Evelyn reminded herself. She hadn't been hatched from an egg. She had been born into her family the natural way. That certainly hadn't resulted in them being a functional family. So the opposite was surely true. She could be an excellent mother to children whether they were biologically hers or not.

With a sigh and the slightly dejected feelings dodging her steps, Evelyn determined to climb up to see whatever was left of the chateau that had once stood upon those cliffs. It would surely provide her with a majestic view and that would have to lift her spirits, or so she hoped. She certainly couldn't allow herself to slip into a depression on her trip. For one thing, that would be such a terrible waste of the lovely experience, and for another, it would be rather too scary to contemplate. With no one there to help her and not being able to properly communicate, she would run into trouble pretty fast if she didn't pull her thoughts together.

"Let it go," she repeated, this time out loud, choosing to ignore the slight feeling of ridiculousness that threatened.

She would have to come to grips with the reality. She and Eric had decided they weren't going to come to parenthood through natural birth. Now there remained adoption and fostering.

They had agreed to try being foster parents even though that would bring them into some heart-breaking situations. Eric had been hesitant. Rightfully so, Evelyn had to accept after meeting with the social workers and case overseers. But still, there was so much need. If they couldn't have their own child, they should surely use their blessings to help others.

They were also waiting to see about the possibilities of adoption. But that was a much longer process. And they weren't going to be getting any younger as that time passed.

Evelyn sighed. She was turning maudlin.

She had finally reached the pinnacle and strode toward the balustrade. Evie stood in awe, staring out over the azure coast in the warm light of the morning sun and gorgeous blue sky. How was something this beautiful even real? And how could she be somewhere so majestic and feel so hopeless?

She couldn't, that was how. Surely this should be inspirational, not something that should lead her to deeper despair. The endorphins certainly weren't doing their job. After the rigorous climb up the three million steps, she ought to be on cloud nine.

She was on cloud nine. Evelyn laughed. Okay, maybe cloud five. Was that a thing? She had finally made it to the South of France, something she had absent-mindedly dreamed of for most of her adult life. It was to be savored, not endured.

Yes, there were children running around the small playground beside the café at the top of the hill. That was natural. Something to rejoice over. Not something to slip into despondency over.

Evelyn ordered another café latte and moved to sit at a table where she could see most of the city without staring at the playground.

Watching children play had never been a source of sadness for her before. Why was it only now that she was being brought to such a state at the sound of childish giggles?

With another sigh, Evie realized it was likely a result of her and Eric's decision to give up on trying for a birth child. She should have anticipated that this would happen. Eric should have anticipated that it would. She should never have agreed to come on this trip alone. How foolish of them both.

Evelyn had never felt so vulnerable in her life as she did in that moment.

She needed to go home.

She would change her ticket. She couldn't stay here by herself. How could she live through it alone?

There was no one to share her thoughts with. No one to share her burden of grief. Even if she wanted to, which she didn't think she even did, but still. Even if she wanted to talk it out with someone, it wasn't even six o'clock in the morning at home. She couldn't call Eric or any of her friends. She barely had any family she could turn to either, and even if she did, they were in an even earlier time zone than Eric. Not that they would care about her feelings. Why would they start now when they never had before?

Really, if she wanted to, she could call Eric. He had told her to call any time. But she was feeling a little mad at him right at the moment. More than a little, if she were being honest. What had he been thinking to send her off on this trip by herself? He had to have known she would be struggling with her feelings.

But she was letting go of anger, wasn't she?

And it wasn't as if he was so very in touch with feelings. And surely he must be having some of his own.

Her feelings were her own problem, no one else's. And if she was so sure her husband ought to have anticipated and supported her potential feelings, had she given even an iota of thought to his?

That idea suddenly brought Evelyn up short. They had both let each other down. In so many ways.

But she was going to do better.

She was on the trip of a lifetime. Yes, it wasn't exactly ideal, doing it alone, or maybe it was. Being alone would allow her all the time in the world to contemplate whatever she wanted. She could do as she wished, think whatever she wanted, eat whatever and whenever the mood struck her.

And she was certainly not going to wallow. She also wasn't going to turn craven and go home at this point.

But she might just want to check on her husband.

Shaking off her doldrums, Evelyn drained the last of her latte and took her cup to the counter before approaching the railing around the edge of the hill once more, looking for the best angle to take a picture to send to Eric. She wasn't that good at selfies but she ought to try to send him one. She thought about taking one of those artsy, moody pictures where she's staring off to sea, but she had no idea how she could accomplish that without a photographer with her.

The thought amused her so she was able to smile quite naturally as she snapped the picture to send to her husband.

Jetlag isn't too bad today. Climbed the hill to appreciate the view.

Send.

He might be up by now, she was reasonably sure if he was going to make it to his office before traffic got too bad, so even if he had forgotten to turn his phone to silent for the night, he shouldn't be disturbed by her message.

Good morning, beautiful.

Evelyn couldn't help the flutter in her stomach at his prompt reply. Both the content of it and the fact that he replied almost instantly. It was almost as though he were waiting by the phone for her message.

Or he had his phone in his hand reading the news or something, she thought with a roll of her eyes.

Want to video chat?

His question had her hand fluttering to her hair in a self-conscious manner before she rolled her eyes again, this time in disgust at her own ridiculousness. She had been with Eric for twenty years. He had seen her in every state imaginable and still tolerated her. Loved her even, or so she had been convinced until he allowed her to go away for a month without him.

Swallowing hard, Evelyn shoved aside her personal issues and agreed to the chat. It didn't matter what her hair looked like. He was her husband. And if it was six o'clock in the morning at home, his bed head was likely worse than hers. With a grin she pressed the reply button.

Chapter Seven

Want to chat? What was he thinking? Eric almost smacked himself in the face at his stupidity. He was still in bed with his hair a rat's nest and his stubbly face all pillow creased.

But he missed his wife. And surely she wouldn't judge him for his morning appearance.

Sure.

Her prompt reply was only one word that didn't convey a great deal of enthusiasm. Or maybe it did. How was he to tell? She used the word *sure* a lot. It conveyed all sorts of meanings depending upon her tone. But you couldn't tell a tone from a text message.

Eric ran a hand through his hair with a heavy sigh. He had asked her to video chat. He better not mess it up by delaying. She'd said in her text she'd climbed a hill, she'd probably have good reception up there, unhindered by buildings. The only place better would be in her apartment, he supposed, but the time zones weren't going to cooperate too well for that.

He waited another beat, wondering if she was going to initiate the call. But when his phone remained silent, he clicked on the video icon and called his wife.

She answered immediately. Wasn't technology grand?

"Good morning," he said, trying to imbue some enthusiasm into his voice. He was glad to see her. She looked great.

"It's afternoon here." She laughed. "I'm going to have to figure out my lunch soon," she added, seeming to Eric as though she were avoiding his gaze, but then she looked directly into the camera and smiled. The sweet, tired smile that he loved seeing in the mornings.

"You look tired." He blurted the words before thinking and wished he could snatch them back. What a way to charm his wife when she was on the other side of the ocean.

"Yeah, I'm not nineteen anymore," she agreed immediately. "All-nighters aren't so easy. It feels like a hangover."

"Take two acetaminophen and a cup of coffee," Eric countered with a laugh, lightening his own mood. "But seriously, how are you feeling? Did the time zones kick your butt?"

"Surprisingly, I think the time zones are fine. I was able to sleep at an appropriate time, thankfully. It's just the remnants of not sleeping during the night of travel, I think. And I'm walking so much, too. But that part's really great, and I'll soon adjust and recover."

There was a brief silence as all Eric could do was gaze at his wife, but it seemed as though she was absorbed in the view in front of her. Not that he could blame her. It was a gorgeous view. But he longed for her attention.

Suddenly, though, she was back looking straight into him, or so it felt, and he felt as though she punched him in the gut with her sad eyes and the words that came out of her mouth.

"There are children everywhere here."

She said it baldly, and the expression that flitted across her face let him know that she hadn't meant to say that. He didn't want to hear it, either. Her grief was exactly why he wasn't with her. But she was his wife. He loved the woman. He needed to support her, especially now. But being so far away made him feel weak and ineffective. He wondered what he could say to help, but nothing came to mind. Suddenly she was all smiles and chattering, taking that question out of his hands.

"The architecture, Eric, you must be so sorry you aren't here. You would love it. And the blues. Between the sky and the sea, there's just so much blue. I don't know how it can be so different from home since we also live at the beach, but somehow it is. Must be something scientific I have no idea about. Light particles or something. But it makes it an amazingly different color. I think people here would argue it's the sunshine but we have the sun at home too, so it can't be just that."

She finally stopped with a little, awkward laugh, and after that came an awkward pause. "How are you?"

"I'm feeling like a heel."

"Oh, no, why?" Evelyn instantly reverted to all sympathy and concern for him rather than herself.

"It was stupid of me to stay home. I ought to be there seeing those views with you." He scrubbed a hand over his face and leaned hard into his pillow.

Silence fell between them for a moment. Eric was surprised. Evelyn had a tendency to take blame upon herself immediately.

"Well, I can't really argue with that." She gave him a small smile and a huff of a laugh that didn't contain any amusement. "But we can still try to both enjoy our time apart the best we can." She paused, looking around herself again before bringing her focus back to her screen. "I will tell you all about what I'm seeing and doing, and you can tell me what you're doing each day." She laughed again, and Eric thought it sounded a little pained. "We'll probably end up communicating more than we do when we're together in person. At least lately."

His heart sank a little more. That wasn't a good sensation. But she was probably right. He tried to force a bit of laughter to match hers.

"Deal," was what he finally said. "You didn't send me any pictures of your apartment. Is it as good as the pictures made it look?"

This time Evelyn's laugh sounded genuine. "They must have had a magical camera because the pictures made it look far bigger than it is. I'm sure Angela has bigger closets in her house than this entire apartment. But it's clean. And in a good location. And since it's just me, it's more than adequate."

Eric was sure she didn't mean to point a finger at him with her words, but he felt them like a stab of accusation anyway. He once again reminded himself of what a coward he'd been.

"I could probably catch a flight, maybe even by tomorrow," he blurted out, watching her face.

She merely stared at him. He couldn't tell if she was happy or sad or bitter or delighted by his suggestion. Again her eyes flickered away, toward where he suspected, after what she had said earlier, was a group of children.

"Has anything changed at work?" she finally asked quietly as she turned her gaze back on the screen. With where her camera was, Eric didn't feel like she was really looking at him, but that was probably what she was doing.

"Not really," he said, not ready to admit there really hadn't been an emergency keeping him at home in the first place.

"Unless you're actually free to come, Eric, please don't do it just because you're worried about me. I'm a big girl," she said the words with a smile that struck him as rather sad but she carried on bravely. "You would just feel restless here if you aren't really ready to be here, and that would likely be frustrating for us both." She paused and looked away again. "I think it's going to be good for me." She straightened herself as though bracing for something before speaking again. "I'm going to *make* it good for me. You'll see," she added with a smile that was a little more like her old self. "I'm going to knock your socks off."

"You already always do," Eric told her sincerely, but she didn't seem to believe his words. She didn't get mushy like she would have years ago if he were to say something like that. Eric again felt that odd sinking sensation in his chest. He needed a hug from his wife and she was across the world from him.

Should he ask her about the children? How she was feeling? Would she want to tell him on a video call in a public place? He didn't want to make her cry. He couldn't handle her tears. Really, he couldn't handle her feelings at all knowing there wasn't a single thing he could do about them. But he did want to know how she was doing. Again he castigated himself for being ridiculous. He couldn't have it both ways.

"What do you have planned for the rest of your day and tomorrow?" was all he finally asked, not wanting to make her uncomfortable. They ought to talk when she was in private about more personal things.

Finally her face lit up in her usual grin. "I need to finish or maybe start," she said with a laugh, "figuring out where everything is in relation to my apartment." She waved a hand as though to encompass her entire environment. "Not everything of course, that would likely be impossible, but I want to be able to get around at least my immediate neighborhood without having to consult the map at every corner." She laughed again. "Very few of the corners are actually square so the streets run off in all different angles. Some are short, some are long. It's fascinating and a bit of a nightmare. But I love it. And that's my plan for today and tomorrow. Just wander around and get a feel for everything." She paused again before adding, "If Rachel were here, she'd probably be imagining that the squiggly streets were designed to evade invaders or something like that. That anyone not from around here would instantly get lost and it's a form of protection. But I think it was just that no one consulted anyone and they all had an opinion and this is the result."

Her laughter delighted Eric. He suddenly realized that he hadn't heard her laugh in a while. Too long of a while. They had both lost something of themselves in the last couple of years. Everything had gotten hard. It would seem Evelyn was going to find some of her missing parts in the foreign country. Or maybe it was just the natural progression of taking a break and refocusing her attention. He would do the same, even if he was too cowardly to do it with her.

He ought to have been by her side, helping her on her journey and getting her help with his own. But like she said, maybe they could still do it together even if they're apart. She hadn't asked him about what he was going to do. But maybe she was afraid to ask, suspicious that he had lied to her about work. She had always used to ask him about work. Now she didn't seem to care.

"How's your work?"

As though she could read his thoughts, she blurted out the question. The uncomfortable expression on her face told Eric that he had been right. She didn't really believe him. Rightfully so, but he didn't want to confirm her suspicions while she was so far away.

"It's getting under control," he said, his stomach in turmoil. It wasn't a lie. But it wasn't the truth either.

"I'm glad," she said, her smile gentle and open, making Eric feel even worse.

"I've been thinking about what I could do for work when I come back. I don't want to go back to my old job. It was too stressful and it was such long hours. I've been trying to think of things I can do from home, because if we—" she stopped for a moment and changed her tone. "When we start fostering, it would be good for me to be home and available to them, right?"

"That does sound like a good idea," Eric said right away despite his misgivings on the topic of fostering. "But only if you want to. Maybe you don't even have to work at all. I bring in pretty good money. And since you've been home, we don't grab take out nearly as often, nor do we need someone coming in to do the house chores since you've been looking after so much of that. So please don't feel like you have to rush back to work. It might even be to our advantage to have you be a stay-at-home wife. You know, with taxes and such."

She made a humming sound and her smile slipped a little. She wasn't nodding as much as she usually did. Eric got the uncomfortable feeling that she didn't quite agree with him, but he wasn't really sure. He couldn't tell what she was thinking. He didn't like that unusual feeling. But he wasn't just trying to flatter her. He had looked at the numbers. Aside from the fertility treatments, which they'd both agreed to paying, Evelyn being home the past six months had really impacted their bottom line in a good way, which you would never expect when thinking of your wife quitting her job.

And his increased focus on work had paid off. He had been pulling in more than ever. So really, Evelyn didn't have to work at all if she didn't want to.

"I did get my degree for a reason," she finally said in a rather dry tone. A chunk of hair seemed to float in the breeze around her face. "But I really appreciate your saying that, Eric. Let's think about it a little more. I'll keep brainstorming my ideas, and we can talk about it again either before or after I come back. I have a feeling

I might not feel like a fully-fledged adult if I don't have some sort of work to do, but it's good to know there isn't the pressure of our bills not getting paid. It will give me the chance to really think about it and make a good decision. Or maybe I'll even just play around with a few ideas until I see what fits well."

He was glad she wanted to talk about something so innocuous. He wasn't prepared to tell her how afraid he was about fostering children, even though he had agreed to it. If she couldn't handle the pain of not getting pregnant, how was his soft little wife going to handle finding out what really went on in the world?

He would happily discuss any other possible topic.

Eric felt much better about the conversation now and would have happily continued, but Evelyn's gaze started to bounce around again. She smiled into the camera and announced brightly, "Well, it's probably time for you to get up and about so I shouldn't keep you. It was lovely to catch up a bit. I hope you have a great day. Love you lots."

Before he could catch her and offer a reply, Evelyn had disconnected their video call leaving Eric feeling deflated and very much alone. And he only had himself to blame.

Chapter Eight

Evelyn stared at her phone. Taking deep breaths in through her nose before releasing them through her mouth, she tried to decide how she felt about the conversation. It was good, right? Asking herself wasn't really going to get much of an answer. Her lips twisted in wry amusement.

It *had* been a good conversation. Even though he hadn't really asked about her feelings when she had revealed them slightly. But what was he supposed to say? He was probably afraid she would burst into tears. In a public place. On the other side of the world. Not a situation her big, manly husband wanted to trigger, Evelyn was sure. He had never been much able to handle her tears, not even happy ones.

But he had tried. She knew he had tried to communicate, at least a little. And his generous offer of being the sole provider. That was kind. Evelyn didn't think she would be comfortable taking him up on the offer, but it did take some of the pressure off her to be successful right off the bat with whatever she decided to do from home.

And if they were given complicated children to care for, which was quite likely, it would give her the option to not work at all, especially if it was a small child who didn't go to school yet.

Evelyn got to her feet from the bench. It was time to continue her exploration. Going to the balustrade, she tried to figure out where her apartment might be, but even with the help of the map on her phone she couldn't be certain which of the buildings below was hers. She would come again when she was more familiar with the streets. And maybe she'd make it for the earlier morning light. Evelyn was certain it would be spectacular.

No matter how much chattering she did into the silence of her mind, she couldn't avoid her thoughts straying repeatedly back to her conversation with Eric.

He had looked a little guilty when she asked about work. But that could be just because it was work that had prevented him from coming with her. Or that had been his excuse anyway. Evelyn sighed even as she climbed down the million stairs that would take her back to the old city. Had it been a believable excuse or had there really been a work emergency? Or was it a cover? What was he really up to?

Not that she really believed he was doing anything nefarious. Eric was a good man. She knew that all the way down to her toes. And she was nearly one hundred percent certain that he still loved her deeply. Maybe not in a hot kind of way like they used to feel, but she knew he would never hurt her. Well, it had hurt to hear him say he wasn't coming on the trip with her, but that had been more shock than injury. And it was likely more to do with his own feelings about their complicated lives than about his lack of feelings for her.

Really, Evelyn might think her husband wasn't taking care of her feelings, but had she really taken any care of his? She had shied away from thinking about this the night before but she really needed to address the issue. If she was going to complain that Eric wasn't offering any care about her feelings, she would be a hypocrite since she hadn't really given any thought to his.

He had wanted children nearly as much as she did. Even more than Evelyn, he cared that they be directly their children, children of their own bodies. It had taken some convincing for him to even consider fostering or adoption. He had agreed to becoming foster parents, in part, because it was temporary. He didn't yet envision taking any children they didn't know truly into their home as part of their family.

Evelyn was going to have to respect his feelings. She was going to have to properly understand them first. Really, what they needed to do, was sit down and really discuss it. Not just in an abstract, here's a possibility we should go for, kind of way, but in a 'how do you really feel about it' kind of way. She should have made sure they did that before they signed all the paperwork and went to the classes. Surely, as two competent adults, they should be able to have that sort of conversation together. They had used to discuss how they felt about everything under the sun. It was only when the hurts started piling up that they started avoiding the deeper conversations.

Well, what felt to Evelyn as the biggest possible hurt in existence had happened to them. They weren't going to have a biological child. That was done and behind them. Sort of, anyhow. She was still living and breathing and even enjoying moments here and there. They would get through this. They needed to learn how to get back to being the couple who talked. Not just chattered but really talked about their feelings.

Once Evelyn figured out her feelings, then she would figure out how to share them with Eric. That was the new goal for her trip.

Yes, it was going to be very cool to see everything there was to see in the beautiful, sunny, south of France. But that was just architecture and scenery. She was going to use this time to figure out who she was and where she was going. And how both of those things synced up with her husband. She was also going to give deep thought to how awesome her husband was and how they could get back to really feeling that about each other.

Starting right now.

Evelyn stood at the balustrade halfway down the chateau hill and stared straight out to sea. She could never tire of the shades of blue and the constant motion. But in that moment, she barely saw the sea. She was thinking about a different blue. The darker, more navy blue of her husband's wise gaze.

She and Eric may have gotten mired in the complications of their infertility journey but that didn't mean they no longer loved one another. It was time to stop wallowing in her grief and figure out how they could be the happy, loving unit they had once been. If she could get over her anger with him, she would get right on that.

And, she might need to wallow in her sadness just a little longer, Evelyn acknowledged with a smidge of a smile as she flinched from the sound of an especially enthusiastic shriek coming from the children's play area above and behind her. It was time for her to get moving again. She had more ground to cover before she went home for another early night of catch-up sleep.

Evelyn soon found herself noticing once more how many couples and families were exploring the city. From what she could tell, she was the only person touring alone. How awkward. Grief and irritation warred for supremacy in her chest. She shouldn't be alone. If she had a child, she'd never be alone, she thought with a sniff.

But was that thought true?

It might be true that she was genetically inadequate to bear a child and for that she could honestly mourn, but children grow up and leave home. That is the natural progression. That's what you want for any child, for them to become fully functional, independent adults. Even if she and Eric had several children, there was still the conceivable possibility that she would be alone at times in the future. That didn't have to mean she was unlovable. Even if it felt that way in the moment.

She ought to be happy for those families and couples, not consumed with jealousy. But she would admit to herself as she snapped some pictures of the happy people around her, she was pea-green with envy. She would try to be happy for them. But that was a project for another day.

Evelyn stopped in a boulangerie and bought a pastry. This was definitely the day for some carbs.

Sitting at a small table outside as usual, enjoying the sunshine, Evie was surprised to be approached by a flustered woman speaking accented English.

"Forgive my intrusion but might I sit with you?"

Despite a slight flutter of misgiving, Evelyn gestured to the chair angled beside her with a smile. "Sure, I don't mind a bit of company."

The other woman smiled hesitantly and took the seat, glancing around nervously.

"My boyfriend was following me."

Evelyn blinked, wondering what she had gotten herself into. The other woman hurried to explain herself.

"I should have say my ex-boyfriend, no? We broke up. But he doesn't let go."

"I'm sorry. Are you in danger?" Evelyn was ready to help but was on shaky enough ground herself. But there was a high enough police presence, she didn't think she needed to worry overmuch.

"Not danger, no," the woman shook her head emphatically. "But I don't want to see him, you know? We broke up. Why should I see him? How could I find someone else if he always is there?"

Evelyn couldn't decide if she really wanted to involve herself in the situation, but it wasn't likely that it would harm her to listen to the young woman. She was obviously in need of a friend or at least a companion.

"How can I help?"

"Thank you. I know I impose. You are very kind. But I knew you would be since you are American."

Evelyn laughed. "How could you tell?"

The other woman shrugged as though it would be impossible to explain. But since it was not an insult in this case, Evelyn didn't argue the point.

"If he sees me with a friend, a female, he will leave. I just don't want to be bothered with him today."

"I'm sorry," Evelyn couldn't help saying. "That must be hard." But a part of her was actually a little jealous. At least this woman's boyfriend was willing to chase after her. He wouldn't send her off on her own to a foreign country. But she was being ridiculous. Obviously being semi-stalked was an uncomfortable situation, not one she wished upon anyone, let alone herself.

"Has this been going on for long?"

The woman shrugged again, not at all helpful, making laughter threaten Evelyn again. But she didn't wish to insult the woman by laughing at her dilemma.

"You could still go to the police, even if you don't feel unsafe. No one should put up with being stalked."

"The police will do nothing except perhaps deport us. It is not a police matter."

"Ah, I see. It sounds complicated." Evelyn's heart went out to the woman even as it shed an altered perspective onto her own worries. With a smile, Evelyn allowed her compassion to overcome her misgivings toward the young woman. "My name is Evelyn, what's yours?"

"Forgive me for not saying so. I am Anastasia."

Suppressing a grin, Evelyn nodded at the woman wondering if she ought to offer to shake hands. Was that too American of her? She wasn't about to lean over and kiss this stranger's cheek as she had seen others doing around her.

"An exotic name for an exotic beauty," Evelyn said before she thought better of it. What a ridiculous thing to say. Anastasia wouldn't be exotic wherever she was from. Thankfully, the other woman smiled her thanks rather than taking offense. Quickly covering over the awkward moment, Evelyn continued. "Have you been here long?"

With a nod, Anastasia answered. "It is hard to remember when I wasn't here, but it is only a few years."

Evelyn started to wonder if the woman might be somehow trying to scam her. With how vague the woman's answers were to every one of her questions, it made Evelyn suspicious. But then she chastised herself for being inhospitable. It was likely a language barrier or perhaps cultural since Anastasia's English was really quite good.

"How can I help you," Evelyn finally repeated a question she had asked earlier.

"Thank you, Evelyn, I think I am fine now. You have been most kind." And with that, the dark-haired young beauty got up and left, leaving Evelyn to stare after her in confusion. She felt mean doing it, but she quickly checked her bag to make sure she hadn't been robbed while distracted by the encounter.

Relief filled her that everything appeared to be intact amongst her belongings. If anything, the odd experience reinforced for Evelyn that she was going to be fine. Yes, she was in mourning. Yes, she had experienced a loss. But she was still a compassionate and reasonably intelligent member of society. She had been willing to assist the stranger but hadn't been taken advantage of in any way.

There was a jaunty lift to her steps as she continued her exploration of the neighborhood around her apartment.

Chapter Nine

The next morning, feeling much restored from another good night of sleep, Evelyn set out for a long hike she had read about. The good thing about a tiny apartment, it was easy to clean up after herself. She had quickly made herself a breakfast of eggs and the rest of the baguette she had bought the night before. Hopefully it would keep her satisfied for a good, long while. With some water and a granola bar in her small backpack, Evelyn felt prepared for the long walk ahead.

The views were glorious and the trek just rigorous enough to feel healthy. Being alone, Evelyn was glad she had thrown pepper spray into her bag at the last minute. Not that it would do her much good there in a sudden emergency, but it made her feel a little more confident despite being on her own.

This was one of the reasons why it was peculiar, even suspicious, that Eric had sent her off on her own—she was usually a big chicken and wouldn't go anywhere by herself, let alone on a lonely hiking trail in a foreign country. Of course, how was Eric to know she would do something so questionable? She certainly hadn't told him she was going to go on the trek.

Her small encounter with Anastasia the previous afternoon, though, bolstered Evelyn's confidence in her abilities to take care of herself. And the breathtaking views and the rhythmic, crashing waves soothed her nerves and she strode along with something resembling confidence, enjoying the long, solitary walk. She did encounter people from time to time, everyone exchanging the requisite "bonjour." It made Evelyn smile when she heard others saying it in as badly accented French as she herself had. Of course, that didn't mean they necessarily spoke English, nor did it mean that she was yet ready to actually strike up a conversation with another stranger, but it somehow made her feel part of a camaraderie. Like they were all merely explorers passing through. She wasn't a pitiful, motherless woman, abandoned by her husband.

Sighing, Evelyn pulled out her phone and started taking pictures. Forcing a smile to her face despite her suddenly heavy thoughts, Evie took some selfies and sent a few of her and the scenery off to Eric. It was the middle of the night where he was, so she didn't expect a reply any time soon, but she felt the urge to include him. Perhaps that was because he had always been her person, maybe it was just a habit, but despite the fact that a good portion of her twisting thoughts could be blamed on him, she still loved the guy and wanted to include him in her adventure.

The bright sun and the soothing cadence of the crashing waves soon had her back into a less tumultuous frame of mind and she could relax into enjoying the venture. At one of her water breaks, though, she did transfer her small can from inside the bag to her back pocket. It would be foolish to leave herself too vulnerable despite her sense of community with the other hikers. It only took one psycho to ruin a good time.

Contrarily, rather than distressing her, that last thought amused her and her mood was finally lightened enough to put a jaunty lift to her step even though she was starting to feel the length of the hike she had chosen.

Perhaps she should have waited until all the jetlag had fully worn off.

But no, Evelyn refused to accept that thought. She wasn't old or decrepit. She could do this hike. Despite its length and the rugged terrain, it wasn't actually that strenuous. She was convinced able-bodied humans had a nearly inexhaustible ability to walk. Especially if they were wearing decent shoes. A quick glance down at her feet reminded her she was wearing terrific shoes—lovely sports sandals she had bought for the trip. They were cute and almost elegant while also completely practical. She had loved them at first sight. And her impulse purchase had not been a mistake. Her feet weren't even beginning to protest the long walk. Evelyn again allowed her gaze to return to its perusal of the rugged terrain. This lovely landscaped trail all along the sea seemed to go on for miles. It did go on for miles, all around the Bay of Villefranche sur Mer. She could see marinas all along the way ahead of her. She hoped to spot one of the Rothschild villas but she wasn't sure if it would be clearly marked. It seemed to her as though the trail could go on forever but she knew it would end at the next lighthouse. It would be the perfect finale for her hike. Or rather the perfect halfway point since she would have to turn around and retrace her steps. But she probably should have brought more than a granola bar as sustenance.

As she walked, Evelyn tried to imagine who had worked on creating this trail. It seemed to her to be an inspired feat. She wondered if anyone had drowned in the making of the trail whenever a wave came particularly close to her. It was a beautiful, mellow day, and still the occasional wave nearly reached as high as the trail. She couldn't imagine how it must have been to work on it, especially if there had been inclement weather the night before, which would make the sea particularly agitated.

Apparently she was in a particularly macabre frame of mind if she was thinking such thoughts. Evelyn chastised herself for being so negative. It was a gorgeous day and a breathtaking vista on a perfectly groomed path. She wasn't going to ruin the experience for herself with thinking bad thoughts.

Stay in the moment, she admonished herself.

Think of the five senses. What are the five senses again? Taste, touch, smell, sight, sound? Is that right?

What can she taste right in this moment? There was still a little bit left over bitterness from her morning coffee. Maybe a stick of gum was in order, she thought with a smile.

What could she touch? Well her hands were empty. But the air was dry and her palms weren't nervously damp despite her earlier fears.

Stay in the moment, she admonished again.

Right, touch. She fingered the soft cotton hem of her t-shirt and then ran her hands down the denim of her capris. Both were cotton but very different textures. Her hands were dry. Could probably use some cream.

Ok, smell. What could she smell? There was a faint perfume of some sort of flower. She was never very good at identifying flowers, especially not by scent unless it was lilac or roses. But it was pleasant and light, not overly musky. There was a little hint of pine in the air, too. Also, the sunscreen she had applied against the heat of the sun. And of course, the lovely fresh sea smell. No rotting seaweed to ruin it. Just a fresh breeze. Her favorite.

Sight. The best sense to have in the south of France. Everywhere she looked was either blue or golden tan. The rocks might be a form of sandstone, she wasn't very sure. They were very jaggedy along the coast with many sheer cliffs, giving a very stark and rugged appearance. The color wasn't bland despite the fact the one could almost call it a shade of beige, which was the most boring color on the earth. But this was far from boring, especially with the varying shades between where it was wet from a wave and turned a deep brown, to where it faded from the sun to a color almost nearing to a shade of white. As far as she could see off to her right were varying shades of blue depending on the depth of the water or where the sea met the sky, changing hues again. In front of her she could see the peninsula she was walking toward. There were trees, people, beautiful houses perched on the cliffs, and the lovely lighthouse she hoped to reach before she starved to death.

Was hunger a sense? It tied in with taste and touch, she supposed. It was time to enjoy her granola bar, Evelyn realized as she resolved to stop at one of the restaurants she spotted in the village she walked through. On the way back it would be the perfect way spot.

She had one more sense. What was it? Oh yeah, hearing. What could she hear? Not a great deal over her own breathing and the constant flow of the waves. The occasional birdsong and the sing song of various languages as she encountered others on the trail. She could hear her own thoughts but thankfully they had quieted down with this exercise.

In this moment, she was content. She was physically turning out to be a little more fit than she had even suspected, which was something to rejoice over, that was for certain. She had been led to believe the trail was going to be a little easier than it was turning out to be. There was more hill climbing than she had expected and way more stairs. But she was managing it perfectly.

She was proud of herself, she insisted in her head but then added a sigh.

Sort of.

She tried to be, in any case.

But it was so hard when she hadn't managed the one thing she should be able to do automatically. Most women don't even try. Half the children she heard of weren't even planned. Why was she the one who couldn't manage it even at great effort and expense?

Another sigh later and Evelyn was doing her best to reel her fraying emotions back in.

Look at the rocks, listen to the waves, deep breath in of the lovely flower-scented air, stay in the moment. Maybe if she said it enough, it would stick.

Evelyn almost snorted with laughter and then glanced around sheepishly hoping no one heard her having a personal moment and thought her to be a lunatic.

Not that it mattered what anyone thought, she reminded herself firmly, for at least the second time in the couple of days she had already been on her trip. Especially not here where she knew no one, but it didn't matter anywhere. She knew who she was. Well, she was going to figure it out any way. But she knew she wasn't a lunatic. And even if she were, so what? If she wasn't hurting anyone, what did it matter? She could snort-laugh to herself whenever she wanted and it shouldn't matter to anyone one way or the other.

Evelyn stopped to take another drink of her water and admire the views. She sure wished she could share them with Eric. With a shake of her head and a roll of her eyes, Evelyn pulled out her phone to send another selfie to the man. It should almost be time for him to be awake. She shouldn't be blowing up his phone but she was reasonably sure he had sufficient storage. And knowing him, he had the right settings so any pictures she sent weren't going to clog up his phone unless he chose to allow it, like if he saved them or downloaded them or whatever.

She could stand there all day and admire the way the light glinted off each incessant wave and then it crashed onto the rocky shore with a splash and a shush. The combination of sound and sight were soothing and hypnotic. Calming.

It was the perfect place to be when your mind was in tumult.

Chapter Ten

"**B**onjour!"

Even she could tell this person wasn't really a French speaker. Evelyn smiled at the couple who had barged into the small alcove she had settled in, just off the trail. Should she bother making the same strained greeting? Or would it be better to say hello? From the looks of the man's socks with his sandals and the woman's sweatpants, Evelyn had a very strong suspicion they were American. They wore bright smiles and appeared delighted with themselves and the world around them. Despite Evie's suspicion that the middle-aged couple were going to get on her nerves, she couldn't help finding them amusing in a cautious way. What if she was exactly like them?

"Isn't it gorgeous?" she finally asked with a smile. They might not actually be English speakers, but she was nearly certain they weren't locals.

"Oh, are you American? How refreshing," the other woman said with a laugh that made Evelyn want to roll her eyes. If you were in a foreign country, it shouldn't be refreshing to hear your own accent. But the woman likely didn't mean any harm. "Are you here alone or are you waiting for your family to meet you?" The woman laughed again. "Or are they waiting for you to catch up somewhere?"

It took even greater effort for Evelyn not to roll her eyes at the woman's insensitive questions.

"I'm doing this trip solo," Evelyn said with a tight smile. "Work emergency for my husband."

"And the kids are too busy with their own interests to come with boring old mom, I suppose?" the other woman added with sympathy. "Our kids couldn't be bothered either. But then we promised ourselves this was going to be romantic." The strange woman must have finally realized she was being rude to Evelyn. Her eyes suddenly widened and she put her hand over her mouth as though to stem the flow of her words.

"My wife doesn't have a filter," the man finally said, with a gentle smile. "And she thinks everyone is in the exact same circumstances as she is," he added with a shake of his head. But Evelyn could tell from the way he gazed at his wife that he loved her despite, or maybe because of, that flaw.

Evelyn's heart squeezed with what she knew was envy. The couple was happily in love and parents to more than one child too obnoxious to accompany their parents. It sounded more than perfect to her. Feelings of inadequacy threatened to swamp her once more, but she swallowed back the tickle of tears that wanted to clog her throat. Without bothering to say anything else, Evelyn nodded and was nearly overcome with relief when her phone rang, eliminating any need to comment further.

"Good morning, darling," Eric's voice sounded as though he had just woken up. "It looks like you're having another adventure."

"Eric!" Evelyn hoped she didn't sound too relieved to hear from him. How could she possibly explain what had happened over the phone?

"I suppose I ought to say good afternoon, to you, shouldn't I?"

"Well, it's morning for you. And I know what you mean."

"Am I interrupting?"

"No, actually, your timing is quite perfect. I could use a little break." She offered what she hoped was a genuine smile to the couple and then turned her back on them, relieved when she could hear their footsteps receding.

"How far are you walking? And have you walked the entire way?"

Evelyn laughed and it felt good and genuine. "I have walked the entire way. There seems to be a great transit system here, but so far, I'm happy to be seeing everything from my own feet. When I'm ready to go farther afield I'll take some sort of bus or train, but for now, I'm enjoying the walking." She glanced at her watch. "So far, I've done four point three miles. I think I have one more to go, approximately."

"Is that when you'll be back to your apartment?"

Evelyn laughed again. "No, that's when I'll turn around and head back."

"So you're planning to walk upwards of eleven miles?" Eric sounded appalled at the very thought. "Suddenly I'm a little less disappointed that I'm not with you."

Evelyn didn't feel much like laughing in response to that and wasn't sure how to respond.

"Sorry, that was insensitive," Eric said right away. "It was supposed to be a joke, but I can see that it was in poor taste. And I don't mean it. I am disappointed I'm not there, not just because your pictures are gorgeous." He sighed and Evelyn could imagine him running his hand through his hair, mussing it up in that adorable way he had whenever he was trying to think a matter through. "I should be seeing it with you, not just through your eyes or pictures."

Evelyn couldn't argue with him. He *should* be there with her. But she wasn't about to rub it in or try to make him feel worse.

"I'm working on staying in the moment," she blurted. "I'm glad you called. I need to notice my surroundings. I can tell you and you can let me know if you can see it or not."

"That's a good idea," Eric said. Evelyn could hear the rustle of sheets as though he were getting into a more comfortable position. "Tell me what you see and feel."

"The breeze has picked up so the water is getting choppier. It's still a beautiful day and since it's just past noon, I'm glad for the wind as it might be too hot otherwise. I feel a little disloyal but I think the blues of the sea and sky are even more beautiful here than at home. Do you think that's just the novelty of it?"

Eric laughed lightly. "Whether it is or not, I promise you Cape Avalon won't mind if you love the beach there a little more than here."

"Oh no, that's not what I said. I just think it's more beautiful. That doesn't mean I love it more."

Eric laughed again. "I stand corrected. I'm glad you aren't so shallow as to base your love on appearances. That bodes well for me."

Now it was Evelyn's turn to chuckle. "It wouldn't matter if I did since you only seem to grow even more handsome with age. It's actually one of the most annoying things about you."

"Why would that be annoying? While I don't agree with your assessment of my looks, thank you for saying so, but why would it be annoying even if it were true?"

"Because I don't share the same blessing," Evelyn huffed in amused exasperation.

"Sure you do. The longer I've known you the more beautiful you become to me," Eric vowed.

"Aren't we the declarative pair today?" Evelyn said with a giggle that stemmed from nerves. She wasn't sure if she could believe what her husband was saying. But she appreciated his words anyhow. "I suppose that's a sign of your love for me. It's making you see me through rose-colored glasses if you think I'm better looking now than I was when we were kids."

"I know you now, way better than I did then. Your heart is the most beautiful one on earth, Evie. I know you could make a ridiculous list of all the flaws you think you have, but no matter what you might come up with, I know there's nothing more beautiful to me than you."

Evelyn's heart felt as though it were being torn in two. She almost couldn't breathe. He was saying the exact right things. But he was on the other side of the ocean. A part of her was melting into a pile of emotional goo. The other part of her filled with a rising fury. She couldn't speak. Silence grew between them.

"Are you still there? Did we drop the connection?" Eric asked, still sounding warm and sleepy. It didn't soothe Evelyn's feelings.

"Then why are you there and I'm here?" she blurted before she could stop the words.

She hadn't meant to ask, but how could she not? He professed to love her, but he sent her on their dream trip alone. She, of course, shared some of the blame. She had agreed to go without him. And without argument or question. She tried to blame her lack of questioning his decision on shock, but she had accepted without even a murmur. Except in her head. She had been screaming inside. But you wouldn't likely have known it from looking at her.

His heavy sigh should have made her feel guilty for asking, but she refused to accept that feeling. She had nothing to feel guilty about. Unless he thought she shouldn't have come when he had changed his mind.

Silence stretched between them again before Eric sighed once more.

"You're right, Evie. It was ridiculous of me to stay home. I regretted it the minute your flight took off. I knew you were trying so hard to be brave and not make me feel badly for not going with you, but I could tell you were disappointed." He sighed again. "And you're still disappointed, aren't you?"

Shockingly, Evelyn actually laughed. "Isn't it better that I'm disappointed rather than delighted to be here on my own?"

There was a slight pause before Eric's rich chuckle filled her ear, causing a little tumble to Evelyn's midsection.

"You do have a good point, there, darlin'," he drawled. "I must say, you're being a better sport than I probably deserve."

Evelyn laughed lightly again. "I'll make sure you feel my irritation in the credit card statement."

Eric's chuckle mingled with hers. She was sure he knew that was an empty threat considering she didn't love shopping.

"I know you aren't the vindictive sort, Evie, so don't bother making threats. But I do hope you find something nice to buy for yourself. And don't scrimp on your fun while you're over there."

"The funny thing is, being on my own, it will probably be far cheaper than if we were here together. I don't really love eating in restaurants by myself nor am I comfortable drinking when I have to get myself home."

Eric's indrawn breath made a hiss and Evelyn regretted her words. She hurried to explain.

"That wasn't meant as an admonition, I promise. More an agreement that I'm not likely to hit you in the pocket book. But I do plan on going to this rather decadent sounding mall near the airport at some point so I might retract my words later."

Evelyn was glad she had explained because she could sense Eric relaxing even from this distance.

"Be sure to tell me all about it when you do." Evelyn nodded at his words even though he couldn't see her and was relieved when he continued, "Have you finished telling me about everything you can see right now?"

"No, I forgot to tell you about the boats. There's a marina, or maybe several, they sort of all blend together but it's likely there are more than one. The trail I'm on goes all around this bay out to a point, so it's probably a brilliant place to park your boat as it would likely be more protected in the event of bad weather."

"Does any of it remind you of the Cape?"

"Not really. Which is odd, isn't it? You would think everything would remind me of home, but even though it's on the water, the two places are quite different. Maybe because it's a sea rather than the open ocean? I can't really say what the difference is. But it's much more rugged here with the rocks. And the shape is completely different. Do you think maybe the sea is shallower than the ocean? Would that make a difference? Who knows, maybe even the longitude or latitude changes things." Evelyn laughed and shrugged even though he couldn't see her. "Doesn't really matter why it's different, it just is, but each has their own charm."

Evelyn was a little embarrassed about the conversation, which was foolish considering she was talking to her husband but there you had it, feelings didn't follow logical patterns.

"Anyway, I probably ought to let you get on with your day," she quickly said.

"And I ought to let you get on with your adventure," Eric countered. "Thanks for sharing it with me. I appreciate getting your pictures. You looked a little sad in one of the ones you sent me earlier though. Are you going to be okay? Do you think you should come home?"

"I'll be all right, I'm sure. Yes, I have many moments where I'm sad for various reasons. But that's no reason to pack up and go home. You could always catch a flight and come here, though, if you'd like. You are allowed to change your mind."

Evelyn got to her feet and hefted her backpack onto her back, so discomfited by their conversation that she couldn't sit still. She tried to cover her discomfort with more words.

"Anyway, just putting it out there. You have a wonderful day. Love you lots." And she hung up. She didn't even wait for him to respond. Her hand had the slightest tremor as she shoved her phone back into her pocket and she set off on her trek once more.

She shouldn't have stopped moving. Her muscles had stiffened up. A little more walking should loosen them back up. Or so she hoped, otherwise she'd be in trouble for the walk back.

Evelyn hoped the frivolous thoughts would prevent her from exploding with her anger. Come home? How could he even think to suggest she come home after all of this? One foot in front of the other. That's how she would get through her anger, her grief, and this gorgeous hike.

Chapter Eleven

Eric stared at the phone in his hand. The silent phone. The one where his darling wife had hung up in his ear after telling him she loved him lots.

Shaking his head at his own thoughts, Eric had to smile at his word choice. No one hung up in your ear anymore. It was an old expression harkening back to the days when a landline phone actually hung on the wall and you could make a very satisfying amount of noise as you ended the connection. With technology, it was much more passive. Or passive aggressive, he thought with another wry twist of his lips. But Evie wasn't ever aggressive. Nor even passive aggressive, unless you counted when she got all quiet. But that wasn't in a misguided attempt at punishing him, he was certain of it. It was just when she felt badly or small or whatever crazy things she felt when she was upset.

It was almost as though she were embarrassed to have asked him to come to France. Why would that be? Had they drifted so far apart that she couldn't even ask him to be with her? Why was she so sensitive to his feelings that she didn't want to tell him hers?

That was the real crux of the problem, wasn't it? They both had so many big feelings they were trying to cope with that they didn't want to burden one another with their own problems.

But he was the man. He ought to be able to carry a greater burden than his grieving wife. And she was grieving, he was certain of it. The fertility clinic had warned them of the grief they would face if they decided to stop trying. They really ought to have gone to the therapist the clinic had suggested. Instead they had planned their trip to France. The one he had reneged on, allowing his grieving wife to go off on her own.

France had always been Evie's idea. She had spoken about it off and on as long as he'd known her. Really, he should have taken her years ago. But they had gotten busy and wrapped up in their lives and he hadn't given it the thought it deserved. Obviously.

When they had made the difficult decision to stop the fertility treatments, it had been an off-handed remark on his part about the savings they still had which had prompted Evelyn to start planning her dream trip. He hadn't objected. She had been so excited about the idea and rushed headlong into the planning. In hindsight, it was likely a little manic on her part, like an overreaction to their sadness with the decision.

It had been the right decision. Eric was confident about that despite how sad it had made both of them. So it hadn't bothered him that Evelyn had thrown herself into the trip idea. It wasn't a bad idea in and of itself. But, at the last minute, he had realized it was grief fueled and dug in his heels. He didn't want to witness her grieving in her dream destination.

He should have gone with her and helped her deal with everything. But how could he help her deal when he didn't even know what he himself felt? He couldn't move forward, so how was he supposed to help her do so? He really was too foolish for words.

But she had said she loved him lots.

Yes, she had said it in that too chirpy tone of voice he didn't like as it indicated there were all sorts of other things being left out, but he trusted his wife. She wasn't lying to him. She did love him. There were just obviously all sorts of other things going on. Things she didn't want to tell him about. And with her on the other side of the world, it was very easy for her to avoid telling him.

He would have to join her. She was right. A vacation away from their usual spots was the perfect environment to work through all their feelings. Or at least for Evie to work through hers and for him to help her, if he could bear it. Eric still wasn't sure what his feelings were, but surely he was responsible for helping her with hers. He didn't know if he could, though.

A weary sigh escaped him. He shouldn't have bothered calling her. It was too early in the day for this empty feeling that was taking him over. He slouched back down in the bed. There was time for him to sleep a little longer.

A few minutes later, though, with a heavy sigh, Eric rolled out of the bed. There wasn't going to be any more sleep for him. His annoying thoughts and his guilt weren't going to allow it. The restlessness of his mind was translating into his body and he knew another early morning jog was the best choice for him in the moment.

He could have worked. That was his usual go-to when his mind wouldn't settle. But he suspected that this time it was far too tumultuous for that. You shouldn't be managing other people's wealth when you couldn't focus your mind.

It took less than two minutes for Eric to toss on his running gear. There was no sense in showering before he went, he was soon going to be a sweaty mess. And eating before jogging was a quick way to getting a seriously upset stomach. Besides, he was a little too riled right now to eat anything, anyway. He would have breakfast later.

He had almost pounded himself into a mindless state when he noticed the sound of heavy footsteps coming up behind him. A quick glance confirmed it was his next door neighbor, Jake.

"You're out earlier than usual," Jake said in lieu of a greeting, already short on breath.

Eric grinned and swiped away a rivulet of sweat, even as he shrugged. He didn't have an answer for the other man.

They jogged side by side for another twenty-five minutes before Jake finally lifted a hand.

"I don't know what's eating you," he heaved out, "but I can't keep up any longer." He slowed his pace, and Eric matched it.

"Sorry, man, I didn't mean to make you run harder than you're used to."

"No worries, my bad," Jake huffed out. "It was pride, man. I didn't think you could outrun me. You have to have at least five years on me."

"More likely ten," Eric said with another grin that might be closer to a gloat.

Jake laughed.

"You okay?"

"Running makes me that way," Eric replied with a nod.

"Well, go on ahead without me if you have more distance you're wanting to get in. I didn't mean to interrupt."

"Nah," Eric said, "I ought to get back and get on with my day. I'm actually glad you interrupted. I had lost track of how far we'd gone."

Eric tried to ignore the younger man's probing gaze as they turned and started a slower pace back toward their homes.

"You haven't stopped by for any grub yet. Evie must have left you well stocked," Jake commented.

"She hasn't been gone long enough for me to go through her supplies yet," Eric agreed.

"You know you're always welcome if you want to join us."

Eric nodded, unsure how to respond. He wasn't about to spill his guts to his neighbor, even if they were on friendly terms.

"Thanks," he finally said with a nod, not bothering to make eye contact.

"From what Rachel says, it seems Evelyn is having a good time in Nice."

Eric almost stumbled. But didn't. He also didn't respond.

"Sorry, man, it must be tough being here and her off on her adventure. If you ever want to share a beer or something, just come on over."

Eric grunted something that might have been an affirmation or acknowledgment. It wasn't likely he would act on the offer, but he knew it had been meant as a gesture of kindness.

They loped along in silence after that. It wasn't an uncomfortable silence. Jake wasn't really the chatty sort; Eric was grateful for that fact. And he had never stuck his nose where it wasn't invited.

Until now it would seem.

Looking uncomfortable, as they slowed to a walk right before they reached their houses, Jake turned to him with an expression of determination on his face.

"Look man, I know we still aren't tight like our wives are, and there's every likelihood this is none of my business, but it seems odd that Eve went without you. Rachel's mad at you for it but can't explain to me why. I figure there have to be reasons that don't necessarily mean you screwed up. If you ever want to talk about it, or just don't want to be alone, please know you can come over."

"Even if your wife is mad at me?"

Jake grinned. "Even if. Worse comes to worse, we can sit on her pier and sip a cold one."

"Thanks, Jake, I do appreciate it. You never know, I might surprise us both and take you up on it."

Jake laughed and stuck his hand out to shake. Eric accepted the gesture and even slapped the younger man's sweaty back in a show of manly comradery.

As he trudged up to his house, Eric had to acknowledge that while the run hadn't been quite the escape he had hoped for, it had still made him feel lighter than when he'd started it. Wouldn't Evelyn be delighted if she returned to find her husband had made friends with Jake?

Chapter Twelve

Evelyn marched as though her life depended on it. Or as though she were trying to escape her feelings, she thought with irony. That was true. But even if she took up running, even marathon running, which she would never in a million years do, there was no way she could outrun the feelings that were threatening to overwhelm her.

The good news was, her muscles were no longer stiff. They were burning from her exertions, but that actually felt good. She might regret it later but for now it was distracting her from the real issue at hand. Her feelings. The sheer volume of them. They were threatening to overwhelm her. But just maybe if she kept marching toward the lighthouse at the point, she could stay one step ahead of them.

It was wishful thinking but since she didn't want to break down into a puddle of grief right there in the middle of a popular, frequently travelled hiking trail, there was little she could do except stay ahead of it, even if she knew it would catch up to her eventually.

Life is full of choices. Choose wisely. They had chosen to stop the fertility treatments that weren't working. They had chosen to apply to be foster parents rather than trying to adopt. Or rather, perhaps in addition — they were still debating that. But, had she rushed that decision? Had her desperation made her choose the faster option? Had she chosen wisely?

Evelyn wasn't certain why those words kept floating through her mind, but it was a welcome distraction. She needed to choose to return to the moment. But she also needed to deal with her feelings. She needed to accept that feelings in themselves weren't "bad."

She had finally caved and stopped to buy something more substantial than a granola bar to eat. She had optimistically thought she could walk all the way to the point and then stop for a meal nearly back to her apartment. But with the way all the restaurants closed for long periods in the afternoon, Evelyn had realized she shouldn't risk it.

"Bonjour." This time the greeting was obviously from a local as she stepped into the small *café*. It smelled heavenly of fresh baked bread and coffee grounds. But they didn't have a great many selections. Her choices looked like sandwiches or sandwiches, Evelyn thought with a smile. But the sandwiches did look delicious. And the granola bar wasn't going to suffice. She had been a little overconfident in her ability to walk well over ten miles without proper sustenance.

Evelyn was tempted to sink her teeth into the baguette liberally stuffed with brie and smoked meat as soon as she stepped out of the bakery but she had promised herself to make it all the way to the end before she took another full break so she carried on.

Finally feeling calmer and somewhat restored to equilibrium, Evelyn reached the end of the trail and had a spectacular view to enjoy as she sat to finally eat the delicious lunch. When she had shoved the baguette into her backpack she had been skeptical of the sandwich holding up throughout the rest of the hike, but from the looks of it as she unwrapped it, she'd been wrong.

Her eyes closed on the verge of ecstasy as she bit into the crunchy softness of the French baguette. The tang of the smoked meat and the creamy cheese made her tastebuds dance with joy. Evelyn almost burst into laughter over her fanciful thoughts but they were a welcome relief after how dour she had been feeling since the phone call.

She shouldn't have hung up on Eric. Not that she had really hung up on him. She had at least said goodbye and told him she loved him. But she had ended the conversation in a manner not at all like her usual way of speaking, especially not with him. She always waited for him to end a conversation.

Not that she needed to do that. Her ending the conversation felt as though it might be a step toward taking back control over her life. She really needed to grow a backbone in all areas of her life. Including how she felt watching other families, she realized as her mouth grew dry when her gaze fell upon a group of children chasing each other around on the beach nearby, their delighted shrieks and squeals piercing her heart painfully. That should not cause her pain. She should find it delightful. It *was* delightful. But it still left her feeling lonely and empty. That was on her. It certainly wasn't the children's fault.

Shouldn't it be getting easier by now?

It had already been three and a half weeks since they had definitively decided to stop their efforts to have a child naturally. Well, not so naturally when they had to use all sorts of injections and medical interventions to even try. But naturally in that the child would have been from her body. From both her and Eric's bodies, really. But now they had finally agreed that they were going to stop all those methods. It had helped slightly that they had already started the process of fostering, but only just barely. She had still been holding onto a last shred of hope that the latest efforts would have worked.

She fought a shudder as she remembered the conversation.

"I don't think I can stick another needle in you, Evie. Don't you think you've tried long enough?"

"No, we haven't succeeded yet," Evelyn had countered taking the syringe from him and staring at it, wondering if she could go through with sticking herself with it. Her stomach turned at the thought, but it would be worth it. If it worked.

"I think it's time to call it, babe." Eric's voice had been gentle but firm. "We can't keep doing this."

Tears had poured down her face but she had held in the sobs. "What alternative do we have? Are you saying you want to give up? Can you be happy with that decision?"

Eric's sigh had nearly bowled her over.

"I think we'll be happier than this, Evie. Can you really say you're happy to keep being poked and prodded and taking needles and medication and then crying your heart out when it doesn't turn into anything?" He'd sighed again. "Because I'm not. I can't take it anymore. I think we need to make some changes."

Evelyn swallowed back the bile that had threatened her then and threatened now. She had thought, in that moment, that he might suggest a divorce so he could find some other woman who could give him children. He hadn't, of course. He was too good a man for that.

When she had come up with the idea of being foster parents, she knew he hadn't loved the idea, but he had signed the paperwork and gone to the classes with her. They were still planning for their own baby at the time. That was why he was reluctant, or so she'd thought. It had been suggested to her by one of the fertility clinic staff, that having a child in their house already might make conception easier. They never got a chance to find out.

They weren't going to bother with the adoption wait-list either, at least not for now. They would try fostering, first. It would be a much quicker way to get a child into their lives. And Evelyn needed a child in her life. A child of her own. Even if he or she was only on loan to her, the child would be hers for the time that it was in her home. Evelyn had been longing for that for as long as she could remember.

A heavy sigh escaped her. A psychologist would have a field day with her if he were to ever examine how desperately she wanted children. It, of course, stemmed from the coldness of her own childhood. Evelyn reflected on the first time she could remember thinking about having children of her own as she watched the little kids frolic around the lighthouse.

She couldn't have been much older than five or six, the same age as some of those kids. She had been in the first grade; she knew that for certain. It'd been the first time she had been exposed to children from other families. That had been the first time she had realized that not all families were like her own. And that was when she had vowed to have a family of her own that she could love exactly how children ought to be loved. And all that love she had been storing up in her heart for the family she was going to have was starting to feel like it was going to ferment if she didn't find somewhere to put it soon.

But they had a plan now. As soon as she got back, the social worker had promised her there would be children needing her. Maybe one, maybe more, it would depend on what was needed at the time. Evelyn didn't really care. She was beyond ready for it.

Still, though, as her eyes tracked the movements of the noisy group of children playing on the beach, it was still a challenge for her to release the desire to have a natural child.

She didn't think it was the genetics aspect. Her own experience assured her that being biologically related to people didn't make you a loving family. So Evelyn was nearly certain that she wasn't completely devoted to the thought of having bio-children of her own. It was just that she was now going to miss out on the earliest stages of the children who would come into her life.

And was she strong enough to help them with whatever they would need help with? That was actually her deepest fear. While her own past equipped her to cope with one very specific childhood trauma—cold indifference—it was unlikely the children who needed fostering would have that exact situation in their own background.

The social workers had assured Evelyn and Eric that there would be psychologists to help them through whatever they needed to get through. Evelyn was determined to take advantage of that provision as often as possible, both for herself and Eric, and for the children who would come into their home. She realized she should have done so before now. She ought to book an appointment, or several, for as soon as she got back. She needed to be in top form for the sake of the children.

The children she hadn't even met yet. But she would. That was certain. Conviction spread through her. She would have children in her life. It was no longer a question. Perhaps she should look at their decision from that perspective. Giving up on trying to get pregnant and signing up to be foster parents actually made it more sure that there would be children in their near future.

Again her eyes strayed toward the noisy group and she was finally able to look at them without feeling a stab to her heart. Perhaps she should try to befriend them?

That might look suspicious or sketchy, though. Would their parents think she was a creepy stalker person? Of course, they would. She would if she were in their position. And she likely couldn't even communicate with them, she realized as she heard more distinctly what the children were screaming.

It wasn't English, but Evelyn suspected it might not even be French. Not that her French had progressed very far in her few days in France, but other than the smattering of phrases of French she had learned, Evelyn didn't know any other language than English.

That had been terribly short-sighted of her. She ought to have taken more of an interest in languages when she was in school. She had studied the humanities; she'd had ample opportunity to take languages in college. Spanish, French, Latin, German, even Chinese. Why hadn't she bothered?

It was likely the English-centric hubris of those who lived in predominantly English-speaking countries.

It didn't matter why. She was not a polyglot, that was certain. And so she couldn't approach the families she was watching. And she ought not make them uncomfortable by watching them longingly, either, she told herself with something that verged on a giggle. A slightly nervous giggle but it was genuine none the less. And it was a start.

Evelyn had been reading about the emotional journey. She knew she was on one. Rachel talked about it often, telling Evelyn that every creative person went through it while developing a project. When Rachel talked about it, it was from an author's perspective, of how a project always ends up being more challenging than expected. But that was just part of the journey. And inevitably there was always a dark moment when you had to decide whether or not to continue.

It seemed to Evelyn that it applied to her situation as well. She wasn't completely certain where she was on the journey. It was possible she hadn't yet reached the dark swamp of despair, that hardest point where you had to decide whether it was worth continuing. Or perhaps she had, surely they had reached that point when they'd decided to stop trying. She hoped she had and was maybe even getting past it. But if she hadn't, it was definitely not something she was looking forward to.

It was possible all the books she had read had it wrong, though. Evelyn was almost certain the journey wasn't nearly as linear as psychologists would like you to think. She suspected there were many despair swamps to grab her before she reached the other side. Or maybe it was just that she had multiple journeys to face.

There was what she was going to do with her life, for one. While she had been absolutely consumed with her efforts at bringing a child into the world for the last several years, she was now trying to accept that there were other things in life. Even if they had managed to have a family of their own, children grew up and had lives of their own. Evelyn shouldn't have invested so heavily in the assumption they would grow a family.

She and Eric needed to return to investing in themselves. Or each other might be a better way of putting it. He really ought to have come with her.

Evelyn needed to stop being such a doormat. She was allowed to be upset with her husband. It was a big deal that they had decided not to keep trying for a baby. Everyone agreed that it was a big deal. Evelyn ought to have insisted that Eric come on this trip. They had agreed together on the trip. She was convinced it was exactly what they needed to get out of the funk they were in. And she was determined to get out of it whether Eric wanted to do so or not.

Except what if he wasn't in a funk? What if he had already moved on with his life? What if he had been waiting to have her out of the house so he could make his moves on changing his own life? Without her.

Evelyn tried to tell herself it was a ridiculous fear. Eric wasn't deceitful. He wouldn't be so crooked as to send her off to France in order to leave her. She didn't think he would ever actually leave her, but if he did,

Evelyn was certain Eric would have the decency to do it to her face.

But she was going to have to ask him about it.

One more swamp of despair to deal with.

Ok. So that's one, deal with not ever bearing a child. Two, confront Eric about the state of their marriage. What was the third? Oh yeah, what she was going to do with her life.

Evelyn had less than no desire to return to the corporate world now that she had been home for more than six months. But she did want to be a contributing member of society. Even if they had their family, Evelyn was beginning to realize she needed to do more than keep house. Not that there was anything wrong with keeping house. It had a certain fulfillment and was absolutely a necessary aspect of life. But she wanted to have as full a life as possible. She wanted more friends than she currently had, and she wanted some sort of career that would give her a sense of pride and fulfillment. She just didn't want it to consume her like her corporate life had done.

Could she solve points two and three together? Should she and Eric try to come up with a career plan for her together? Or could she possibly do something complementary to what he did?

What did she really know about what Eric did? She knew he was in stocks and trading, following the markets and funds and such. Evelyn knew the jargon, but she didn't really know what exactly went into it.

While she wasn't sure if she wanted to devote herself to that sort of work as it seemed to her to smack too much of what she wanted to leave behind, it would do her good to ask Eric about it. Even if she didn't decide to work with him, just knowing more about what he did would surely help toward shoring up their flagging marriage.

Because it was definitely sagging in the middle. Her friend Rachel had become a successful novelist and often talked about the saggy middle of her stories. Evelyn was pretty sure that was where she was at in her story. But that could only mean the best was yet to come.

Chapter Thirteen

One step in front of the other was the way Evelyn made it back to her tiny apartment. She had stopped now and again to admire the varying views. The sunshine glinting off the waves somehow seemed different from one side of the bay to the other as she made her way around it. Evelyn wasn't sure if that was because the sun angled differently with the passage of time or if it was an east or west thing. Whatever the reason, it fascinated her.

The bustling marinas she marched through had been briefly captivating along the journey as well. The furling sails, the revving motors, the calls in varying languages from crewmen to shore were fascinating to both the eyes and ears. But nothing could quite fully distract her from her heavy thoughts.

Despite her near constant admiration for the views, Evelyn's mind had been heavy with her concerns. That likely explained why it felt like a bigger workout than it ought to have been. Really, eleven or twelve miles wasn't that big of a deal, was it? True, she wasn't in the habit of such long walks. But it was a walk none the less. It shouldn't leave her feeling as though she had run a marathon.

Evelyn hoped to do that hike again, maybe with an earlier start time so she would see the angles differently again. She also wanted to spend more time photographing the boats and people. And with a little more food in her backpack from the beginning. Or maybe not. Despite her pack being rather light, Evelyn was weary down to her bones.

Every muscle quivered with fatigue as she climbed the stairs to her apartment, watching her steps closely as the stairs weren't perfectly even. She didn't like to hold the railing in public places, but today she made an exception due to her jiggly legs. She'd have more to worry about than germs if she were to trip and fall down the stairs.

It was probably the emotions she had carried around with her. It was time to take them to task. She had pushed them around and held them off long enough. It was time to talk to Eric.

A quick glance at her watch told her it was only two o'clock in the afternoon at home. She had dithered at the lighthouse, stopped for an ice cream in a little town square, and taken her time returning to the apartment. Now it was evening for her but only early afternoon for Eric. Would he be able to talk?

There was only one way to find out.

A deep breath fortified her before she scoffed at herself. She shouldn't need fortification to talk to her husband. She pulled out her phone and hit the little green phone image under Eric's name.

"Hello!" Eric answered after only one ring, his rich voice a little less warm and welcoming than she had been hoping for. "I didn't expect to get to talk to you again today. Is everything all right?"

"Yes, yes, everything is fine," she quickly assured him, trying not to let annoyance drift into her voice. "Is this an okay time for you? I know the time differences are a bit of a pain for us to be able to have a good conversation. It's either too early for you or you'll be too busy."

"No, no, I'm not too busy. I'll never be too busy to take a call from you, you know that."

His voice sounded like he was chiding her and Evelyn tried not to take exception to his tone. She blew out a breath.

"Well, I meant, do you have time for a real conversation?" Evelyn could hear a slight edge creeping into her voice; she tried not to be mad but she wasn't in the mood to be patronized.

There was a beat of silence before he replied in a more careful tone. "Of course."

"Are you certain?" Now that she'd started it, Evelyn wasn't really sure if she was ready to go through with it. Could she really have a heart-to-heart conversation with her husband over the phone from six time zones away? Her patience had worn thin with him. Would it make things better or worse to talk it out on the phone?

"Tell me what it is, sweetheart. You sound nervous. You're dithering. You know I love you. You can tell me anything, I promise."

His voice had gotten soft and gentle and all Evelyn wanted to do was cry. But that wouldn't solve anything. Somehow she was even more irritated by his words. Why couldn't he have been this supportive when she was still at home? Maybe she should wait and discuss this face to face. Evelyn blew out a frustrated sigh. She needed to stiffen her backbone and get on with it.

"What was the emergency that kept you home?"

Evelyn suspected they were both surprised that this was the question that came out of her mouth. She hadn't even known she was going to ask that. She didn't really want to know. What if he really was having an affair? Even if he was, ignorance wasn't really bliss.

No. Eric wasn't having an affair. He wasn't trying to leave her. There must have been an actual emergency. Or some other reasonable explanation.

His heavy sigh didn't bode well. Evelyn could hear the sound of a door shutting and then the creak of his office chair as he sat firmly. She should have called him on a video chat.

"Could we see each other? Do you mind switching to video?"

Without answering, he did as she asked. She should have combed her hair or put on some lipstick. She was windswept and tired. But that didn't matter. Eric looked like he had been kicked in the gut. He looked tired and defeated. She was torn between worry for him and anger that he hadn't told her.

"I'm sorry, Eric. I should have asked you sooner. Is it something very stressful?"

He raked his hand through his hair looking even more dejected. Slowly he shook his head. Evelyn frowned, confused.

"I'm sorry, too, Evelyn. It wasn't anything terribly serious. Not something worth my staying home for, in any case."

Evelyn blinked and stared. "What, what do you mean?" she stuttered out, uncertainty roaring through her.

Eric blew out one more heavy breath before he looked her straight in the eyes. "I was a coward, Evie. I felt as though all I've done is let you down for the last three years. All I'm good at is making money, not babies."

"But the doctors said it's my fault, not yours."

"I don't believe that. It can't possibly be your fault, sweetheart. You are everything that is perfect. It can't be your fault. It must be mine."

Suddenly Evelyn was laughing until tears were streaming from her eyes. Just when she thought she had herself under control another gust of laughter would overtake her. She was deeply insulted and yet somehow also touched by his words despite everything.

"So I'm beating myself up and you're beating yourself up and neither of us are actually blaming the other, so we're a world apart and feeling miserable for no reason?" She finally managed to ask the question once she'd gotten herself a bit under control. She knew it wasn't really funny. She wondered if this was what hysterics felt like.

"It would seem so. I've been a complete idiot."

"Maybe a little," she couldn't help agreeing. "I really should have gotten you to talk to me before I left. But, to be honest, I was afraid of what the answer might be."

"What did you think was a possibility?" Eric frowned, confusion evident on his face.

"So many possibilities taunted me, really. I thought for a beat that you might be having an affair or thinking about leaving me. Or maybe you were just sick of your failure of a wife."

"You are not a failure!" He nearly shouted the words but rather than making her feel badly, they made her feel stronger, as though the force of his feelings invigorated her.

"I'm trying to see that. But it's hard," she admitted with a soft sigh of her own. "Do you think you could get away and join me here for the second half of my trip?"

"I'll try," he said, not making her any promises.

Evelyn didn't push the matter. She still wasn't done being mad at him, and she was still trying to figure herself out.

"Was there actually a problem with work at all?"

She surprised herself by persisting on that topic. Her mouth actually dropped open and she almost called the words back. Almost but not quite. This was part of her growing a backbone. She needed to start somewhere. And she had promised herself she would resolve the distance between herself and Eric or there wouldn't be a marriage to go home to despite their love for each other. This seemed like it might be able to both contribute toward her growing in her strength of character and shrinking the distance between her and Eric.

She wasn't sure if she ought to be dismayed or delighted when Eric shook his head. Both, she supposed. At least he was being honest with her. But too bad the truth was that he had been dishonest with her before.

She held his gaze, not flinching or dismissing the topic. She also didn't rush to fill the silence as would have been her usual reaction to such a situation. Her impulse was always to fill the silence. But silence could mean someone was just thinking. She had to allow Eric the chance to think his way through his response.

"There was a little issue with one of my funds. But it wasn't such a big deal that it couldn't have waited a few hours or even a day. Or I could have maybe managed to get it resolved before even leaving. In any case, it's mostly taken care of now." Eric raked his hand through his hair and lowered his head dejectedly. "I'm sorry Evie. Another way that I've let you down."

Evelyn stayed quiet until he finally lifted his gaze and looked at her. Then she shook her head. "You didn't let me down. Well, that's not true. I am disappointed that you felt that way and couldn't be honest with me about it. I thought we had talked extensively about this trip so I am shocked to find out you didn't want to come, but that is your right. I'm having a good time, though, even if it might be better to have someone with me." She drew a deep breath, fortifying her strength, and continued.

"Can you tell me why you didn't want to come? Do you even know? Or was it just kind of instinctive?"

Eric raked his hand through his hair again. Evelyn suspected he wished he could pace. She felt the urge too except that her feet and legs were much too tired. The fleeting thought lifted her spirits slightly as it held a tinge of amusement.

"It isn't really that I didn't want to go. In fact, I really do wish I could have seen all those amazing places that you're seeing. But I just couldn't do it. I couldn't stand to face your grief for another day. And this trip you're on, even though you say it's beautiful and you're having a reasonably good time, it represents your loss. I thought for sure you would end up hating it for what it represents. And I just couldn't do it. I thought it might be good for both of us to get a break from it, you know?"

Evelyn bit her lip and nodded, willing her eyes not to well with tears as they seemed always inclined to do these days. Why couldn't he have just stood by her side a little bit longer? A mingling of grief and anger nearly closed her throat. "I sort of understand. And I can sort of see why you would think it might be a good idea to take some time apart. I don't necessarily agree. Or rather, maybe we should have chosen to take a breather somewhere a little less dramatic," she added with a small laugh. "And maybe cheaper. I really do wish you could see all these amazing places."

"I know, Evie, as I told you, I was an idiot."

Evelyn shrugged and shook her head. "Not an idiot," she said firmly. "But you should have told me what you were thinking. We need to be honest and share with each other or we're not going to survive."

"Have you told me everything you're thinking?" Eric asked in a challenging tone that made Evelyn laugh again.

"Of course not. That is not my strength. But we're starting fresh, I've decided. Starting now. We really should have gone to see the shrink the clinic suggested," she added with a soft sigh. "That probably would have helped." She let her breath out slowly but then shook her head once more. "Never mind. I'm trying not to wallow. Let's just promise each other to try to share our thoughts and feelings a little more diligently in the future, okay?"

"You're being remarkably calm about this," Eric said with a frown. "I'm not complaining, but I'm finding it a little strange."

Evelyn laughed. "I can understand that," she said, nodding. Her gaze skittered around the room before she drew it back and tried to meet Eric's eyes. "The thing is, I *am* grieving. Quite intensely, in fact. You know that already. That's why you didn't want to be here with me. You probably are too, although maybe not as badly as me since it seems like the desire for motherhood is both an emotional and a hormonal thing for women. But I'm sure you've got feelings you're either dealing with or ignoring. I was trying to ignore mine. But they keep sneaking up on me here. I wonder if it's the isolation because I don't speak the local language and I'm here alone."

"I'm sorry, Eve," Eric started to say, but Evelyn cut him off.

"That actually wasn't a complaint. I think being forced to confront these emotions is a good thing. Trying to ignore or run away from feelings doesn't really help them from what I've seen. They just fester. So whether you're here or not, I think we should talk, really share with each other. Or maybe we should find a therapist. Maybe even online, right away while I'm gone. I don't really know. For sure when I get home, though." Evelyn's laugh held a note of nerves. "I haven't a clue, really, what I'm talking about or what is best. But I know

I still love you and I want us to be stronger than we were before, definitely stronger than we are now. We aren't really in a good place, are we, Eric?"

He was quiet for a beat but then shook his head. "No, I guess we aren't." He didn't look fully convinced but Evelyn was glad to see he didn't appear to be as defeated or downtrodden as he had been. She so rarely stuck with her intentions when she wished to point out any issues in their relationship. Any time she actually did, he didn't receive it well, becoming defeated before they ever got anywhere. Somehow, she had managed to convey to him this time that it wasn't her intention, that she wasn't blaming him or pointing fingers. Despite her intense sadness about so many things, she was rather proud of herself for that.

"What do you suggest we do about it?" Evelyn asked. "Or rather, should I ask, do you want to do anything about it?"

Eric's heavy breath almost rippled her hair even though he was on the other side of the ocean. Evelyn thought about smiling over her whimsical thought but it was too serious a moment to do so.

"Evie," he said heavily. "You know I love you, don't you? Of course, I want to do something about it. But I just needed a break from all of it."

"Even me, Eric? You needed a break from me?"

"I can't deal with the fact that I haven't been able to give you what you've always wanted."

"But we've found a work around, haven't we?" Fear and sadness cramped in Evelyn's belly.

"Have we?" Eric asked in a tone that sounded weary to Evelyn's ears. "I know I signed all the paperwork and went to those classes, but I don't know if we should go through with taking in foster children. You know all the possible outcomes they told us about in the classes. I don't think you can handle it."

Evelyn was stunned into silence.

She stared at her husband on the phone's small screen and thought about throwing the phone across the room. She thought she was going to be sick to her stomach. She had been too easy-going about this whole situation, and she knew it. But deep down, a storm was brewing, and she couldn't ignore it any longer. She needed him to feel the weight of their strained marriage.

"I think you're wrong," Evelyn began, trying to hold to the shreds of her composure. "But we have to both agree. It wouldn't be fair to the children to bring them into a house of division." She took a deep breath and let it out slowly. "I think I have to think about this some more. I don't agree with your conclusion, but I suppose I have more than my share of blame for why we've gotten where we are. I have been rather single minded of late."

"I'm not trying to point fingers, Evie."

She tried to smile at him to show she understood, but she didn't really. "I still wish you had told me all this before I left."

"Do you want me to book a flight right now?"

Evelyn shrugged. She was surprisingly ambivalent about it at the moment.

"I would have loved to share this experience with you. But I understand better now why you decided to stay home. You have to decide for yourself if you're ready to be here with me. I'm still in the process of grieving and if that's too much for you, then maybe it's better that we have this time apart, as you said."

"Wow, Eve, the water must be different over there or something."

Evelyn smiled, but it felt wobbly. "Why do you say that?" she asked even though she was pretty sure she knew what he meant.

"You're different. You've only been gone a few days and already I can see that you're learning to speak for yourself."

"I guess it's all the time thinking. And a full stop in my regular routine, too." She tried again to appear pleased. "Anyway, I'm pooped from my day but it's still the middle of yours. I should let you get back to whatever you were doing. I'm glad you've finally shared your thoughts, but now I need to go."

Eric's eyes widened and he straightened up. "Wait a minute, Evie. You aren't about to hang up on me again, are you? You still haven't explained why you did that this morning."

"I didn't hang up on you," she grumbled.

Eric just looked at her with his eyebrow lifted in that adorable way she loved, expressing skepticism and doubt. It made him look like one of the dukes in Rachel's historical novels.

"Well, maybe I did end the call a little abruptly, but I wasn't hanging up on you."

Eric's voice softened along with his face. "What happened, sweetheart?"

His warm tone melted her a little as it always used to. "There were so many families and so many feelings. I just had to move, you know?"

"You were trying to get away from your feelings?"

At her nod, he bit back laughter. "Did it work?"

Evelyn shrugged. "A little, sort of. I got in a really hard march for a bit and it helped me work some of them out or through or however you ought to say it. I guess I just mean that I really do understand why you didn't get on the plane. It was sort of like me walking a million miles today."

"Not exactly the same, but I see how you'd make the comparison," Eric said, with another heavy breath and a hand shoved through his thick hair. "What a pair we are, aren't we, Evie?"

"We used to be a perfect pair, but now I'm not so sure. I'm here trying to stop wallowing in my grief and you're home avoiding it." She tried to laugh lightly but she wasn't sure if she managed it. "I'd like to think we'll figure it out. We're just in the swamp of despair right now. There's nowhere to go but up."

Eric's chuckle was brief. "Swamp of despair, huh? Is that from the Princess Bride?"

Evelyn laughed a little too. "I don't think so. It's the emotional journey. It's the low point before things get better."

"Descriptive," Eric commented with a smile.

"The thing is, Eric, I'm not really sure about all of this. I don't know if we can get past your letting me go off to Europe by myself."

Eric's face turned somber, realizing the gravity of Evelyn's words. He sighed heavily, searching for the right response. "I understand, Evie. I messed up, and I'm sorry. It's just that . . . I couldn't bear to face your grief anymore. This trip, as beautiful as it might be, represents everything we've lost. I thought maybe a break from it all could give us some perspective."

Evelyn's gaze softened, but her voice remained firm. "I appreciate your intentions, Eric, but we can't build a stronger marriage by running away from our problems. We need to confront them head-on, together. We've been avoiding the hard conversations for too long, and it's tearing us apart."

Eric nodded, his gaze filled with remorse. "You're right. We've been hiding behind false smiles and avoiding the truth. I don't want to lose you, but I don't know how to fix what's broken."

Evelyn took a deep breath, her voice tinged with vulnerability. "I don't have all the answers either. But I know that we love each other, and that's a good starting point. We really should consider seeing a therapist when I return. It could help us navigate these complicated feelings."

Eric's expression softened, a glimmer of hope in his eyes. "I'd be willing to try. I want us to find our way back to each other. We can't let our grief and doubts define our marriage."

Evelyn managed a small smile, although it felt fragile. "That's what I want too. I believe we can get through this, but it will take effort from both of us. Let's promise each other that we'll be more open, more honest, even if it's uncomfortable. We can't afford to keep these walls between us any longer."

Eric's shoulders slumped with a mix of relief and weariness. "I'm relieved to hear you say that. It won't be easy, but I'm willing to try. We need to find our way back to each other."

Evelyn smiled slightly and nodded before a huge yawn overtook her, surprising her with its ferocity.

"You really did walk yourself into a slump, didn't you?" Eric asked, his eyes twinkling with amusement. "I suppose I ought to let you get to bed. Have you eaten properly today?"

Evelyn lifted a shoulder in another negligent shrug. "Not really, but sufficiently that I'm unlikely to decline into malnutrition any time too soon."

Eric smiled. "I'm relieved to see your sense of humor is returning. But don't get too lazy about proper eating. If I'm trying to look after myself, you better do so, also."

Evelyn rolled her eyes and gave him a mock, melodramatic sigh. "I promise, I'm eating fine. But what about you? I had meant to get more things made up for you in advance but time got away on me. You're pretty much fending for yourself now, too."

"In this, absence definitely will be making the heart grow fonder. Since I haven't had to cook for myself in so long, I've grown complacent about everything you do around the house. I forgot how much work it takes to get a meal properly prepared."

"Rachel would be happy to feed you now and again," Evelyn told him, reminding him of their neighbor.

"I know, but I'd hate to be a third wheel with the lovebirds."

Evelyn laughed. "That's why I said now and again. If you asked, I'm sure they'd happily have you the whole time I'm away, but I'm sure that would get annoying for all three of you."

"I'll be fine. I studied engineering besides finance, I really ought to be able to manage a few well-rounded meals while my wife is off finding herself."

Evelyn tried not to take offence, but his words didn't sit well with her. She hadn't chosen to go on this trip alone. She wasn't here finding herself. She had intended for them to find each other in France. But so many truths had already been revealed in their conversation, she didn't feel like calling him to account for his wording. She yawned again, this one not quite as real as the previous one.

"I have to go. I'll talk to you soon."

She didn't bother to wait for him to reply. She couldn't deal with any more right then. Evelyn ended the call and then stared at her phone as a small smile flirted with her lips. He didn't like it when she ended the call. Maybe he could stew a little bit in that.

Chapter Fourteen

Finding herself? Was that what he really thought? That was absolutely not how she saw it. She ought to have said something right away, but she was afraid she would say something she would regret. She needed to think it through before she reacted.

But she hadn't come to France to find herself. Or had she? And why did his saying so make her so cranky?

She had never meant for the trip to be her own journey of self-discovery. Her intention had been for them to find each other. That had been the plan all along. They were supposed to be together, learning to love each other in their new reality. But Eric had changed the plan without consulting her. So maybe she *would* find herself. He shouldn't be sarcastic about it, though, considering it was his fault.

Evelyn grinned despite her disquiet. She had never been the sort to blame anyone else. It was another new leaf. But maybe a good one if she didn't make a habit of it. Her tendency was to take the blame upon herself. But how healthy was that? And was that why she was so irritated by his saying she was finding herself? Like she had to excuse herself if that was what ended up happening?

As Dr. Phil famously asked, "How's that working for you?" She didn't think it was. It probably never had, but she was certain it wasn't working for her anymore. And she was determined to change it.

She wasn't going to be a doormat anymore. A backbone was required. She wasn't taking the blame for everything.

Her tendency wasn't Eric's fault, though. Yes, this particular situation of being in France alone mostly was his fault, but her long-time lack of backbone was also to blame. He might be able to help her with the situation, but it was likely one that had existed even before he had known her.

Like everything in people's psychology, it probably stemmed from childhood.

Hers wasn't the worst ever, she was sure. She hadn't been beaten or starved. Her family had been sufficiently prosperous, she hadn't lacked for much of anything physically. But she had certainly been neglected. Emotionally and mentally, not physically. Evelyn was becoming increasingly certain that was where the strength of her desire to be a mother stemmed from— the desire to love a child the way she had never been.

A wave of grief threatened to swamp her and she shook her head to dispel the spiraling thoughts. The child didn't have to be biologically hers to be loved by her. She was fully convinced of that. And she was nearly completely convinced that they would soon have a child in their lives. They had been approved. But Eric wasn't as on board as he had led her to believe. Maybe not nearly completely. Semi-convinced, she thought with a little laugh.

And then Evelyn sighed. They needed to talk about this some more. If she couldn't convince Eric that she was strong enough to face the rollercoaster of fostering, he wasn't going to be able to go through with it. If he wasn't actually on board with fostering, she needed to know before she brought a poor abandoned kiddo into their lives and home.

But she was going to give herself some grace for a few days. She felt a little raw, like a bruise or a wound, that needed to heal a little bit before she started poking into other areas. Besides, after her long walk that day, she was exhausted. She needed a good sleep and a couple days of not thinking so hard about such emotional things.

***

The rest of her first week flew by. Evelyn explored museums, and markets, side streets, and shops. She was loving Nice and wasn't even overly bothered being by herself. At least that's what she told herself. Out loud. So maybe she needed some company.

"I like this one."

"*Moi aussi.*"

Evelyn nearly expired on the spot from embarrassment. She hadn't meant to say it out loud. Or hadn't realized she had done so, rather. And certainly didn't expect to have someone respond. She turned to apologize to the older man, but he just nodded and waved away her apology with a smile.

The artist's style was not to her taste but he was world-famous as an artist from Nice. She wasn't completely sure why he was so famous. The paintings didn't seem all that great to her. Why was he so fixated on goats? It made her a little uncomfortable. But she supposed he did make excellent use of colors. She just clearly wasn't a modernist.

She was still enjoying her trip to the art museum, though. She really needed to expand her mind on all topics, even the arts.

Her side street wanderings were much more in line with her current tastes, but there too, she had found herself talking out loud.

"How am I supposed to find myself? I didn't even know I was lost."

"Do you mean that literally or metaphorically? I can show you on the map."

If embarrassment was a disease, Evelyn would have died at least half a dozen times on her trip so far.

"I'm so sorry, I didn't realize I was thinking out loud. Thank you, I'm fine." With a slight awkward laugh and a wave, Evelyn hurried away to drown her discomfort in caffeine at her favorite café and considered how to find some real live company for herself.

She signed up for some local cooking classes. It was something she was sure she would love but didn't think Eric would have been into, so it was the perfect thing to do on her solo trip. They had been talking every day. Good conversations. About more than just the weather and the beautiful blues in Nice. She felt absolutely convinced that they would be fine. Well, their marriage could be fine. But they were at a crossroads as to where their actual lives were going. Could their marriage survive in the face of their disparate wishes?

"I still think we should wait until we can move along on the adoption lists, babe. After what we've been through the last few years, I don't know if you're ready for the ups and downs of fostering."

"I'm stronger than you think," Evelyn had insisted, trying not to seethe.

"I know you are," he'd said, trying to seem reasonable. "But why put ourselves through pain we don't need?"

"Because those children need us to," Evelyn replied, trying not to sound sulky or get emotional. It would support Eric's point if she were to burst into tears during the touchy conversation.

"All right. How about this? Let's take it on a case by case basis? I know this is important to you. And I did agree to give it a try. Let's promise each other to keep the honesty free flowing. Let's try it, take the first child they offer to place with us and see how that goes. But you have to agree to accept my word if I say I think it's too much for you."

Evelyn didn't want to agree to the way he was wording it, as though she were an emotional wreck that couldn't bear up under the burdens of a small child. But maybe he could see what she couldn't. And he sounded so reasonable.

"That sounds fair," she'd agreed, happy that they had found a compromise they could both live with. Or so she hoped.

It still bothered her that she was on her wonderful trip alone, but she was starting to see that there were benefits to it. And one of the things she'd hoped for, them getting back to one another, seemed to be happening whether they were on the trip together or not. Despite the time differences, they were talking throughout the day. And Eric was finally sending her pictures too. He had started jogging more.

Evelyn grinned as she remembered when he had told her about it.

"Seems to me, with all your walking, you're going to be in pretty good shape when you get home. I've got to keep up."

"You've always been in better shape than me," Evelyn had protested.

"Probably not anymore. I've been wallowing in ice cream along with you, most nights, remember."

"Well, I'm still doing that," Evelyn said with a laugh. "Maybe not the wallowing part, but there is definitely a great deal of ice cream and pastry happening over here."

"Well, I have nothing else to do," Eric had said with a shrug. "And if we're going to have kiddos bigger than infants in our home soon, we're going to need to be in shape. We don't want to be outrun by the young'uns."

Evelyn laughed as she was sure had been his intention, but her heart had squeezed almost painfully even though she had been thrilled by his words. If he was speaking so freely about them and even planning for getting in shape for them, then surely he was looking forward to the prospect of children in their home. She still hadn't talked further with him about his true feelings on the subject after they had agreed to take one child, but she was so happy about his saying so that she had to clear her throat to get past the emotional clog and carry on the conversation.

"Don't get too hot, though," she admonished, mostly teasing, but partially meaning it. "We still need to match when I get home."

Eric had chuckled and scoffed at her words, but Evelyn knew he was pleased by her backhanded compliment. A contented sigh escaped her as she thought of it on her way to her first cooking class. She was eager to meet her classmates and enjoy the experience.

She felt a little self-conscious being on her own and entering an unknown situation, but she was forcing herself to not think about it. There was no other way to have the experience and she didn't want to miss it just because she might not be comfortable. There could always be the comfort of a pastry later.

She hoped they would learn to make pastries, she thought with a grin. She should have scoured the website more carefully, maybe she would know what they would be doing if she had done so. But she hadn't really cared. All she'd cared about was the fact that the instruction would be provided in English. She had been practicing every day and she did feel that her French was improving. But she wouldn't be able to follow a class in that language any time soon.

"Welcome everyone!" The slim woman facing the gathered, awkwardly mingling group clapped her hands and gestured for everyone to approach. Her speech was only slightly accented and Evelyn found herself relaxing. She hadn't even realized she had been so nervous until her concerns dissipated.

"I am Lucie and I will be helping you learn to cook some beautiful local dishes. Some of you have only signed up for tonight, others have requested several classes. Tonight, we will be cooking ratatouille and coq au vin, two of the easiest and best-known French dishes. If you stick around, we will eventually get to make croissants. So we shall see."

Evelyn almost laughed at the woman's words. Was she trying to tempt the others to stay longer? Eve wasn't sure how many classes you had to attend before you could learn croissants, but she certainly hoped she could do so. She was surprised they would be learning two dishes at a time. That was both challenging and reassuring. Reassuring that it wasn't going to be a particularly basic class.

She had made ratatouille before but wasn't even sure what coq au vin might be. And even with the ratatouille, making it in France and in a class was likely to be a far different experience than what she had tried. Anticipation filled her. This had been a good choice.

A couple hours of chopping, slicing, stirring, and tasting later, they all had their dishes ready for sampling. Evelyn almost laughed out loud at the amount of food. She wouldn't have to cook for a week since they were all to take their leftovers home and it was only her to feed. She was all the happier with her choice.

Of course, if she was coming back in two days, she might end up with too much food eventually.

"You know your way around a kitchen," Lucie remarked as Evelyn was cleaning up her space, much more comfortable with the strangers she had met now than when she had first arrived in the industrial kitchen space.

Evelyn laughed and shrugged. "I cook for pleasure. But I've never taken any classes. This was really fun."

"I think you will be here Thursday too, no?" the teacher asked.

"I will, yes."

"We shall consider pastries then," Lucie said with a nod. "Not croissant, but quiche and tarte."

"I'm looking forward to it!" Evelyn exclaimed.

"You have moved to our country?" Lucie asked.

Evelyn shook her head even as she waved to some of the students who were leaving. "No, I'm just here for a vacation."

"Your companions did not wish to cook?"

Evelyn sighed. It was the unavoidable question. Everyone always wondered how she could have wound up in Nice alone.

"I'm traveling by myself this time," she said, trying not to reveal her true feelings as she did so. She had just met the pleasant Frenchwoman, no need to unload all her angst onto her.

"Ah, my brave, new friend. What have you seen or done so far in our beautiful city?"

Evelyn grinned. She *was* brave, wasn't she? She had stuck to her determination to see the lovely coast even if Eric chose not to come. And she was having a great time.

"I've done so much walking," Evelyn started with a chuckle. "I walked to the lighthouse at the end of Cap Ferrat. That was amazing."

"You must be very fit," Lucie marvelled.

"Nah, I took all day and then slept for twelve hours," Evelyn countered with another chuckle. "I've also visited a bunch of the museums—Matisse, Chagall, MAMAC."

"But of course," Lucie nodded.

"And then this morning I went to Eze. I took the bus there and then walked halfway back. If I didn't need to be awake for this class, I would have walked all the way as I'm so in love with the coastal views. I might do that before I go home."

"Again, I must marvel. You are both fit and brave."

"Not really, but I'm working on it."

"Have you been to the wineries?"

"No," Evelyn said, intrigued.

"I will take you," Lucie declared.

"Oh no, I couldn't impose."

"What is this impose? Are we not to be friends?"

Evelyn laughed. "Thank you, I would love to see some wineries."

"And since you are fit, we will do by bicycle. That will be fun, no?"

Evelyn wanted to say no. Walking was far different from riding a bicycle. But in her bid to be both fit and brave, she didn't back out of the woman's offer.

"That does sound fun."

"Is tomorrow too soon? Or is Friday better for you?"

Evelyn opened her mouth but wasn't sure what to reply. Suddenly she felt as though the woman was a whirling dervish. Another chuckle escaped her but this time it sounded a little more like a nervous giggle.

"I take a group at ten both days so either is good for me, you choose."

Ah! This was another of the woman's business ventures. Suddenly Evelyn didn't feel as though she were imposing on her.

"I hadn't yet made any definite plans for tomorrow so I would love it. Thank you."

"*Bien!*" The Frenchwoman clapped her hands, as Evelyn was realizing was typical of her, and then handed her a business card. "Be at this address no later than nine forty-five so we can fit you for the bicycle."

"What do I need to bring with me?"

"Nothing," Lucie declared airily. "It will all be taken care of. But make sure you are dressed comfortably with good, safe shoes and a sweater in case we are in breeze or shade."

Evelyn wondered if she ought to ask about the cost but then she shrugged mentally. She hadn't been spending much and Eric had told her to spend however she'd like. The cooking classes had been reasonably priced so it was likely the tour would be as well. Even if it wasn't, she was too intrigued to mind much at this point.

Chapter Fifteen

Who was she and what had she done with her former self?

Evelyn asked herself that question as she gazed into the mirror while getting ready for that day's adventure. She had already done a load of laundry which was now hanging on the lines outside her window, and cleaned the small apartment. She had also written up and mailed the postcards she had been meaning to send home to her friends. They had been texting every day, with pictures, but she thought they would enjoy the personal touch of a postcard.

There was nothing left for her to do but set out on her adventure.

And she was determined to enjoy every second of it. The sky's brilliant light told her it was going to be another day of gorgeous weather. Her heart and footsteps felt lighter than they had in years. And she was almost feeling ready to make some new acquaintances. The class the night before had been enjoyable, despite, or maybe even because of, the strangers she had met.

She had no idea how many people she would be encountering today. But she almost felt ready for even the most intrusive questions about why she was on this trip alone. She was on an adventure, that's why.

Evelyn shook her head and grinned at her reflection, delighted to see the sparkle in her eyes and the tan on her face. Her thinning face. She wasn't sorry about the weight loss that was resulting from all the physical activity. And it was a relief to note that there weren't too many wrinkles being left behind as the pudge receded from her cheekbones. Not that she had been too heavy. It had been one of the things she had been very conscious of during their efforts to conceive. Her weight had been monitored closely for the last three years. But as she had succumbed to disappointment, she had started to soothe her feelings with treats. The results had been chubbier cheeks than she was used to.

But that didn't matter. What really mattered was that she was feeling so much better about everything. Not to be melodramatic or anything, she thought as she rolled her eyes at her reflection after one last glance.

It was true though. She hadn't even realized how down in the dumps she had been until she started to feel better. It wasn't just about the baby. Or lack thereof. It was everything. Her appearance, her marriage, her friends, her career. Evelyn had been down about it all. Now, after a week of daily distanced chats with Eric, Evelyn was fully confident that they could be great again soon. Maybe they even already were. They had always been a solid couple, but the last few years of her own single-mindedness had put a bit of a crimp in their bond. She wasn't going to take all the blame, but she would fully admit that she hadn't paid much attention to anything Eric might have been going through or thinking.

That had all changed during their phone conversations while she was here in France. They had talked about so many things, chatting about future plans, past occurrences, Eric's work, work ideas for Evelyn, adventures they might have together and once they had some kids in the house. But were they actually going to have those kids in the house?

That had been a massive relief. When Eric had expressed his feelings about fostering, Evelyn had fully relaxed for the first time in likely years.

"I admit I'm still nervous about it," he'd said one afternoon while she'd video chatted with him from the beach. "If we had a baby, we'd have months and years to get to know him or her. These kids will come to us with personalities and experiences we won't know anything about. And it will likely be negative experiences if they're in the foster system. I don't know if I'm ready for that. I don't know if *you're* ready for that either."

Evelyn had sighed and nodded. That was her fear too.

"But it's just a challenge. And they need a good solid experience. We can give them that. I'm very nervous about the baggage these kids will have, but there are things to be excited about too," he'd said with a sleepy grin from his place propped up in bed.

Evelyn had returned his grin. "What are you most excited about?" she'd asked, curious to hear what he'd say.

"Well, that same baggage-less baby would take years to be big enough to really play with. Even if they give us a toddler, it'll be less fragile and more fun than a tiny baby. But if he or she is even bigger, we'll be able to play sports, go swimming, fly a kite, go to Disneyland. Really, the possibilities are endless."

Evelyn grinned at the memory of his excitement. She hadn't even realized he had so many ideas of what to do with a kid. Despite some of their friends having children, Evelyn realized that they didn't really spend a great deal of time all together. Evelyn herself spent time with the wives and mothers, often without Eric. She hadn't watched him interact with children in years. They always talked about children in more of an abstract way.

His excitement was contagious and Evelyn found herself almost wishing she could go home and get started. But that wasn't healthy, either. She really did need to learn to live in, and enjoy, the moment, the current moment, not continually wishing for something else. And this moment was pretty great.

She was off on another adventure. She would be touring a couple wineries by bicycle. It sounded strenuous but fun.

What a surprise to find out they were electric bicycles. Evelyn laughed when she arrived and saw them.

"What is funny?" Lucie asked as she placed her hands on her hips.

"I thought we would literally be cycling. I expected to be worn to the bone by the end of the day."

"Don't be deceived, though, my friend Evelyn," Lucie said with a dramatic swipe of her hand through the air "The electricity is merely an assistance. You will still work."

"Sure, I don't mind." Evie shrugged. "I'm just thrilled to find out that there is some assistance. It will surely be much more fun this way."

"Of course." Lucie gave her a dramatic wink, making Evelyn laugh again. She loved the confidence of the French. She only wished she could adopt it for herself.

She was definitely adopting it for herself, Evelyn told herself firmly. That was one of the choices she was making here in France. She would fake it until she made it. She was going to be a confident person. She lifted her chin to punctuate the decision.

Lucie clapped her hands as was her habit, drawing the attention of the milling people. Trying to be unobtrusive, Evelyn looked around at the others, gauging how the day would progress. No one looked particularly fit nor particularly unfit for the adventure, so it should be reasonably comfortable for all of them.

And no one looked particularly difficult to please. It would be a pleasant day.

Lucie was helping each "guest," as she called them, get appropriately fitted for the bicycles with helmets and explained how the electric bicycles worked. Evelyn tried to pay attention but was too distracted by her excitement. Things were looking so bright. She had been in France for ten days and was already starting to feel comfortable. She could find her way around the rabbit warren of streets in the old city and was able to order in cafés, restaurants, and the butcher shop without needing to consult her translation app. And she no longer burst into tears whenever she saw a family with small children.

Pride swelled her chest. She was doing it. Independent for the first time, perhaps, ever in her life. If one didn't count her isolated childhood. That wasn't true independence. It hadn't been her choice and she'd had no control over it.

But here, in France, she was actually growing comfortable in her own skin. It was a delightful feeling. One she would look forward to cultivating and experiencing further.

The afternoon with strangers was going to be one more step toward doing just that.

And it turned out Lucie was right about the work of riding the electric bicycle. It wasn't work, per se, but it wasn't the simple sit and enjoy experience that she had been expecting. It was certainly far easier than if it was a pedal-powered bicycle, though. While she believed she had become much more fit in the last ten days, there was no way she would have been able to comfortably ride the distance they did on the electric bicycles.

What a great way to see the countryside! Everywhere she looked, Evelyn marveled over the scenery. It was evident that the seasons were different in this part of the world. It was still early spring back on the Cape with only buds and leaves starting to grow, but in Nice it was the full growing season already. Evelyn admired the lush beauty as they rode by. If she had been powering the bicycle herself, she would have been far too focused on that to admire anything.

Soon enough they arrived at the first winery they would tour and taste. Evelyn listened attentively to the explanations offered by the tour guide, fascinated by their descriptions of soil acidity and air quality, all the reasons why in France you don't order your wine by the grape as you do in America, but by the region in which it was grown. She nearly laughed out loud at how disgruntled some of her fellow tourists appeared by that. She never ceased to be amazed by how ego-centric some tourists could be.

Evelyn had to admit that even she had that tendency. Everyone related to everything from their own perspective, of course. So even when in a foreign place, it was instinctive to compare to what one was familiar with, either favorably or not. But still, when provided with the explanation as to why something was done a certain way, it was more than silly, it was downright rude to disparage it to a local's face. Especially something like local wine. Why not just take their advice and enjoy what they suggested? It certainly wasn't about to ruin anyone's vacation.

But, on the other hand, Evelyn reminded herself, she was far from an expert. She had a tendency to enjoy any food she hadn't prepared herself, and wine was just an added bonus to make the experience even better. She had never considered herself an expert in anything, particularly not food or wine. She supposed if someone did consider themselves an expert and then came to find out they were only an expert in their own environment, that would certainly be disconcerting. She strove for compassion and sympathy. But still fought the urge to laugh. Perhaps it was the excellent red wine she was sipping that was contributing to her mirth.

"Are you okay?" Lucie asked with a smile.

Evelyn blinked over the question.

"Do I look like I'm not okay?" she asked with a frown, causing an answering frown to crease the other woman's forehead.

"Is this not a good question?" Lucie asked, puzzled.

Evelyn stared for a beat and then burst into laughter.

"I'm sorry, Lucie. Where I come from, this question implies that you're not looking okay. It's more an expression of concern rather than a greeting. But I think you just directly translated a generally acceptable French greeting, didn't you? I think, *ca va bien*, right? That directly translates to it goes well. So not exactly 'Are you okay', but close enough." She laughed again but then sobered. "I'm sorry, that was a very long-winded expression that didn't even answer your question. Yes, I'm perfectly okay, thank you."

Lucie's smile demonstrated that she wasn't completely convinced of Evelyn's sanity, which set her off in another fit of giggles.

"I think the wine is very okay," Evelyn said by way of explanation and Lucie's smile spread into a grin.

Feeling relaxed, most of her anxieties and inhibitions relaxed along with her, Evelyn tried to mingle with her fellow adventurers. There was a couple from Texas who were feeling even more out of place than Eve had felt when she'd first arrived so she did what she could to set them at ease.

"We're only here for three days, so we aren't going to make it our home or anything," the younger woman had drawled in answer to Evelyn's efforts. "But you're a peach for being kind to strangers," she'd added. "What brings you here on your own? You're much more adventurous than I could ever be."

Evelyn grinned. "I'm at a bit of a crossroads in life and I needed some new perspective. It's been a good experience so far," she answered lightly, not bothering to go into the details with the strangers who didn't seem to need her ministrations.

There were three young women from New York who were having the time of their lives, but also had no intention of assimilating into the local culture at all. Evelyn introduced herself to everyone, received a bit of information from each, and wasn't asked to share much of her own story. She didn't mind in the least. Her story was odd, she knew, and didn't need to be shared. But from what she could tell, she was the only one staying a little longer in the area, and also the only one really looking to connect with the local culture or atmosphere. She accepted that with a mental shrug. She supposed that was really what tourism was, kind of like going to the zoo. You look, you admire, but you don't become one of the residents.

"You are different, no?" Lucie remarked when Evelyn returned to where she had left her bicycle and backpack, as they prepared to head to the next winery.

Evelyn grinned. "I would usually say I'm ordinary and boring, but it would seem I might be wrong in that assessment."

Lucie clapped her hands lightly, not to draw the others' attention but to express her delight in Evelyn's words.

"You are the least boring American woman I have met in too long."

Evelyn grinned. She loved how some French people expressed themselves in English. And she appreciated the guide's words.

"You're kind."

Lucie shrugged and nodded but added, "And honest," along with another smile before calling to the others. "Come, it is time for us to continue."

There were some groans from several as they got back onto their seats with bruised tushes. Evelyn hadn't sat on a bicycle in decades and she was feeling the discomfort. It would have been far worse if they had been pedaling for power, she was sure. At least with the electric bike, you only had to pedal as an almost instinctive means of keeping your balance. It was still a physical sort of activity but far less so than if you were powering the thing yourself. It was a brilliant way to see the countryside and she was thrilled with her decision to join this excursion.

"Ride with me, Evelyn," Lucie invited, as she was nearby. "There isn't too much traffic here, we can ride side by side."

"Sure," Evelyn said, happy for the possibility of some conversation.

"Are you still having a good time?" Lucie asked, interested.

"Five out of five stars," Evelyn replied with a grin.

Lucie laughed but shook her head. "I am not looking for a good review. I am wondering how you are doing."

Evelyn nodded. "I'm still doing great. And that isn't the wine talking," she added with a bit of a laugh. "I never would have pictured myself on this kind of adventure, but I'm immensely pleased with it. Thank you for inviting me."

"Of course. Is France very different from where you come from?"

"I want to say yes and no. I live on an island, so there are similarities. But, it's actually quite different. It's smaller, of course, and it's very much a beachy, kind of retired place. People live there and go elsewhere for their adventures. This is where people come for their adventures. Am I making any sense?"

Lucie nodded but Evelyn could see that she was only being polite. It prompted another light laugh.

"Tell me about you. Have you always lived in Nice or are you from another part of France?"

"I grew up in Normandy but have been here for fifteen years. It is home. My daughter and her father live here so I live here too."

Evelyn's heart cramped for a brief second but she ignored the sensation, nodding encouragingly for the other woman to keep talking.

"We must share our daughter so it is easier to be close by."

Evelyn's heart stuttered slightly but she kept her smile in place. She couldn't reject every possible friend who had children. Besides, she was the new light and breezy Evelyn who wasn't wallowing. "How old is your daughter?"

Lucie's smile widened with pride. "She is twelve."

"Is that a tough age nowadays?" Evelyn asked. "For me, it seemed like the worst age in life."

Lucie laughed out loud. "I think maybe it still is. But we haven't seen thirteen yet, so I can't be sure."

Evelyn joined in with the guide's laughter until the next question dried her throat.

"What about you? Do you have children?"

"Not yet," Evelyn said, lifting her chin a little as she said that and allowing a slight smile to touch her lips. "My husband and I have just been approved as foster parents."

Lucie's eyebrows rose and her eyes widened. "Foster parents?" she repeated. "This is when you take children in need for a short time, yes?"

"It might not necessarily be short, depending on the needs, but yes, that is a pretty good description."

"You are a very brave woman, my friend."

Evelyn laughed. She didn't see herself that way, but perhaps she should.

"I have a lot of love to give to a child."

"That is a beautiful way to think, Evelyn. You will do much good," Lucie said before her eyebrows lifted again. "I suppose your husband had to stay home to prepare, but I am surprised, after knowing you a little, that you would come on this trip alone. You don't seem the sort to be traveling alone. What has brought you here like this?"

Evelyn couldn't blame Lucie for being puzzled. It was a puzzle. She had to laugh. The alternative, crying, wasn't to be borne.

"It is quite out of character, you're right. But we planned this trip as a way to transition from our old life into our new life. It was actually a good choice. I'm ready."

Lucie still seemed a little confused but didn't press for further information. That was a relief to Evelyn. She suspected she would have had to cry a little if she had. And it wasn't that sort of day or occasion. Evelyn was doing her best to carry on stoically. She was determined to succeed. Not just stoically but with an actual, genuine smile on her face even if there wasn't true joy in her heart yet. It would get there.

It was already there, Evelyn insisted to herself as she smiled into the wind created by the electric bike's speed. She wasn't just faking it until she made it. It was impossible to be anything but joyful on a day like that. And really, her life was pretty terrific. Both the temporary one here in Nice and the permanent one that was waiting for her at home on the Cape.

Chapter Sixteen

Evelyn's backside was starting to protest the day spent in the "saddle." She didn't regret it in the least, despite the discomfort. It had been a good choice. The day was almost done, though. Or rather, the excursion was. They were on the final ride back to where they'd first met.

All the tourists were much more mellow and subdued than when the day had started. It was all the sunshine, wine, and sensory overload of the views, besides the work involved in controlling the electric bikes they had been given. One would be excused for thinking it should have been a very easy day, and it mostly was, but Evelyn was still going to sleep as though she had walked for miles on end. Perhaps it was just all the fresh air. Or the wine. Not that she had sampled very much. But as someone who so rarely drank any, it was surely affecting her at least a little.

It had been a wonderful day. It had also been an emotionally draining day. That many people, not really of her choosing, hours on end, it was the first time since she'd taken her leave from work in order to focus on her pregnancy project that she had been in the company of strangers for that long.

She would live to tell about it, she thought with a small smile that stretched wider as she realized she ought to be proud of herself. She had made friends. With strangers. Friends she was likely never to encounter again, except for their guide who she would see at her next cooking class, but still. She had very definitely stepped outside her comfort zone.

It had been a near-run thing when Lucie had told Evelyn about her daughter, but in the end, Eve was happy for her friend. Truly. And had managed not to go into a decline with the knowledge. Again with the funny historical language, even in her thoughts. Perhaps she needed to widen her reading pleasure to other books than those written by her neighbor, she thought with even more amusement.

But decline or not, she had enjoyed the day with all its various emotional implications.

Evelyn's phone pinged as she was swinging her leg around to climb off the bike. Thinking it might be Eric looking for an update on her day, Evelyn quickly swiped to awaken it. Disappointment swept her when she saw it was just an email, but that was quickly followed by a flutter of nerves when she saw that the email was from their social worker.

Quickly shutting the phone without reading the message, Evelyn shoved it in her pocket and tried to ignore it as she said her goodbyes to her day's companions.

"Would you like to grab a coffee or a drink or supper or something, Evelyn?" Lucie called before Eve could get away.

Evelyn opened her mouth to say "no" but then quickly shut it again. Whatever it was, it couldn't possibly be an emergency. The social worker knew she was away, or rather she thought both McConnells were away, but that meant she couldn't expect them to take a child for a few more weeks. The email could keep. It wasn't as though Evelyn could call or do anything about whatever it might contain in that very moment. She would deal with it later. For now, some cheerful company would be welcomed.

Two and a half hours later, after sharing one of Nice's famous super thin pizzas overlooking the beautiful sea, Lucie leaned back in her chair and smiled gently at Evelyn.

"This was *magnifique*. I never spend leisure time here in the old part. I really should do so more."

"Why don't you?" Evelyn was curious.

"Firstly, because things do cost more," Lucie responded with a light laugh. "Secondly I suppose I usually associate it with work so I tend to stick to the neighborhood where I live or near my daughter's school."

Evelyn nodded, barely even blinking over the mention of her guide's daughter.

"Are those neighborhoods very far from here? Can you still see the sea from there?" She almost giggled over her homonym sentence but managed to hold onto her composure.

"Sadly, no, and this is why I ought to spend more time here. I think, after a while, one can take this view for granted. But spending time with you has reminded me."

"I'm glad I've been good for something," Evelyn countered with a smile. She ignored Lucie's sharp stare. She hadn't meant her statement to sound as insecure as it did. While she still cringed under the one thing she hadn't been good for, she wasn't so self-deprecating that she thought she was good for nothing. Just not the things she had previously valued. She was trying to adjust.

"Tell me about your daughter," Evelyn prompted.

"Are you certain? This is not painful for you?"

Evelyn appreciated the other woman's sensitivity but she was determined to overcome her own. "I will soon have children in my life. I need to learn more about kids older than babies. I can't get pregnant but we tried for a long time. I was so focused on having an infant, I didn't really think about what happens next. I guess I figured I would learn as he or she grew. But now I will need to be prepared."

"This is wise," Lucie agreed with a firm nod. But then she seemed to get lost in thought. "My precious Sophie has just turned twelve years old," she finally said. "She thinks she is nearly a grown up, though. It is very hard at this stage. And I think having her parents not married anymore makes it more challenging for her, even though her father and I have done our best to stay, what is the word, civil?"

Evelyn had to laugh over the other woman's dubious expression. "Has that been challenging?"

Lucie huffed and rolled her eyes. "*Terriblement*," she said with feeling before laughing. "In reality, not really all that bad, most of the time. Especially now that I'm over the hurt feelings from the beginning. But Sophie still holds out hope that we will reunite. That will never happen, of course, so we do our best to keep her satisfied despite the complications." Lucie suddenly sighed again and reached out her hand to cover Evelyn's. "It is for this reason that I think you are terribly brave. My Sophie has really not faced any true difficulty in life and yet she is troubled at this age. So your children are sure to be even more so if they have been forcibly removed from their home. It is very likely you will be blamed by them."

Evelyn had to listen carefully to understand the other woman's words given her lovely accent and sometimes convoluted way of expressing herself. For that reason, it took her a second to understand exactly what she meant. When the meaning struck her, Evelyn was shocked to feel determination rather than despair well up in her chest. She was looking forward to helping the, as yet unknown, children, even if it was going to be difficult at times. To both their surprise, Evelyn laughed.

"I'm sure there will be challenges. But I also think your daughter is at the worst age in life, so even if your home life was completely perfect, she would give you as much trouble as she could think of. That is the way of things, I believe. I do hope we get a little bit younger children than your Sophie, but I feel like Eric and I can handle most situations. Thankfully, the system does provide a fair bit of support, especially for first timers like us. And we will have the resources to get the help we need."

Lucie shook her head and stared at Evelyn with widened eyes. Somehow, Evelyn still maintained her determination and was even able to laugh a little.

"Don't look at me like that, Lucie. These are children we are talking about. Unless they suffer from serious mental deficiency, they are resilient learners. While I am very sure there will be tense moments and lots of emotions, I'm also sure with patience and love we will be able to get through the rough patches and have many good moments."

"Very good," Lucie said, changing her aspect and nodding firmly. "You will do well, I too am certain of it."

Evelyn raised her eyebrows and laughed again. "Were you just testing me?"

Lucie lifted a shoulder as though to dismiss Eve's question, making Evelyn laugh again. There was nothing else for it. What an odd scenario. Evelyn chose to change the subject rather than take the other woman to task.

"What are the other must-see places near here in your opinion?"

"Eze," Lucie replied instantly, as though she were just waiting for Evelyn to ask. This time Evelyn swallowed the laugh that was bubbling in her chest but also held back the eyeroll she so desperately wanted to offer. The French seemed to Eve to have even more hubris than Americans. They certainly were proud of their cities and countries. "Ah, no, you already went there, no? You said so last night, I think, no? Eh bien, Cimiez."

"And what is Cimiez?" Evelyn had to ask as the one-word answer hadn't told her anything.

"Excuse me," Lucie apologized. "I should recall not everyone on the planet has heard of the beautiful garden. And it is possible you saw it already. Did you already visit Matisse? It is very nearby to this museum. An old monastery and the very beautiful gardens. But I think you must drive there, not walk as you have been doing. You are doing too much walking, Evelyn, you will find yourself asleep on the side of the road."

Evelyn found the French way of saying everything is "too much" highly amusing but didn't want to laugh at her friend's language skills. Despite Lucie's quirky expressions, her English was still much better than Evelyn's French.

"Sadly I missed it when I was at the museum. No worries, I will happily return. But I cannot agree with you that it is too far to walk. I very much enjoyed my walk there the first time."

"You are very strange." But she said it as though full of admiration so Evelyn took no offence.

"Perhaps a little," Evelyn agreed with a light laugh, feeling more relaxed than she could ever remember feeling in recent memory. It was odd because she was definitely outside what she would have considered her comfort zone. And still she was happy. Very clearly the trip had been good for her.

Would she have made this much progress if she hadn't come alone?

It wasn't a comfortable thought. But she would like to think she would have done so. It might have been even faster or better if she were making the progress with Eric. She *was* making it with Eric, she reminded herself. They were talking so much on the phone and actually discussing their feelings, she couldn't claim her newfound emotional equilibrium wasn't at least in part with his help. So she was confident she would have made as much progress if he had come to France with her. It would, of course, have been quite different, but it didn't mean it would have been worse or better.

In either case, progress and growth were progress and growth. They were to be lauded, not questioned. She was grateful. She'd been right. Getting herself into a different environment was a good way to incite rapid change. But she was really starting to long for home. And that could only be attributed to the fact that Eric wasn't with her. Surely if he were there, she wouldn't be wishing for home so soon. She hadn't even been gone two weeks yet.

Chapter Seventeen

Finally, after sipping on cappuccinos and then taking a walk along the promenade, Evelyn took her leave of Lucie and made her way back to the little apartment. It had been a great day. She felt as though she had turned a corner and was truly able to enjoy herself in the lovely French city, even if she was by herself. She couldn't say she minded her own company. She was quite good company if she did say so herself. Even Lucie seemed to think so.

She grinned as she climbed the stairs to her fourth-floor apartment. Or third floor, she thought with a puzzled shake of her head. In France they consider the first floor to be floor zero, so that made the floor her apartment was on the third. How could something so fundamental be different?

Reflecting on the day, Evelyn realized that she hadn't once felt a pinch of envy whenever she saw families with children that day. There might have been a twinge of something negative when Lucie had been telling her about Sophie, but Evelyn was willing to excuse that one moment. Instead, now, whatever Evelyn did, she could imagine herself with a child. Not the infant she had always envisioned but a small child, possibly already talking, maybe even already in school, but still very much in need of a loving home to care for his or her needs. And it was a great scenario to enjoy in her mind's eye.

If it was a boy, Evelyn could picture him running on the beach with Eric trying to catch a football or baseball. With a slight shake of her head, Evelyn corrected herself. Even if it's a girl, she might be interested in sports. That would still be Eric's job, as Evelyn had absolutely no skill when it came to anything that required catching. Unfortunately, her hand-eye coordination, or lack thereof, had made her rather unskilled at sports. But she was looking forward to being a sidelines cheerleader. She would happily yell encouragement while the others ran around. Or she would learn, Evelyn reminded herself, thinking of the pastry class she was going to attend the next evening. She didn't believe anyone was too old to learn new things. And she would happily learn whatever she needed to help the children who came into her life feel fulfilled and cared for.

That thought, as she was unlocking the door to her apartment, reminded her of the email she had received and not read. Evelyn couldn't believe she had calmly sat through a visit with Lucie while there was an email from her social worker burning a hole in her pocket. Her stomach fluttered. She glanced at the clock. It was still the middle of the day at home. Maybe she should call Eric and read it together with him. Nah, maybe it was no big deal. She was likely making a mountain out of a mole hill. Perhaps the social worker was just touching base for some reason, letting her know about some course or seminar. Perhaps it was a perfectly innocuous form letter.

After taking a deep breath, Evelyn sat down to read the email.

Dear Ms. McConnell,

We regret to inform you that your application to be a foster parent has been denied. We thank you for your interest in helping children in need, but we will not be able to accept your assistance in this way. We wish you all the best in your future endeavors.

Sincerely,

Child Services

Evelyn stared at her screen. Was it a hoax? A cruel joke? No, surely not. Evelyn stared at her screen numbly before her stomach pitched and she ran to the bathroom and lost the contents of her belly. Shakily rising to her feet, Evelyn felt on the verge of hysterics. A quick glance at the clock told her it was almost four o'clock in the afternoon on the east coast. Would she be able to reach him? What was Eric doing right this minute? Had he received a similar message? Who should she call first? Gloria or Eric? She certainly wasn't going to be able to sleep until she had done something about the message.

Holding her stomach, Evelyn flopped onto the bed and allowed her feelings to be expressed in a fit of weeping. She cried until there were no more tears, but then she forced herself to get up and calm down. After washing her face and brushing her teeth, Evelyn put on the coziest, most comfortable clothes she had brought with her and curled up in an armchair in the living area.

There had to be some mistake. She shouldn't carry on so. Forcing herself to reread the message a couple of times didn't really make her feel better, but she realized there had to be an error made somewhere along the way.

For one thing, they had already been approved. The email being addressed only to her was also a red flag. All previous correspondence had been to both her and Eric. Besides, since they'd been approved, they had a specific social worker. Evelyn had been in semi-regular communication with Gloria for several weeks throughout the process. Surely, she would have had the decency to communicate with her personally if something had arisen that somehow disqualified them at this stage of the process. But the email was from the Office of Social Services, not their social worker.

There had to be a mistake. Surely it was a miscommunication. An error. Evelyn was certain there was a child in the system just waiting for her and Eric's home. This couldn't be taken away from them. And if they didn't qualify, how could anyone qualify? They were stable, financially sound, had a nice home, what could possibly disqualify them?

Unless it was her solo trip to France.

But how could they have found out about it? And why would that disqualify them? Especially out of hand, without asking for details. They couldn't possibly be that conservative or restrictive in their requirements.

It took a while, but after a cup of tea and several more convincing diatribes, Evelyn finally had herself calmed down enough that she thought she could call Eric without going into a fit of hysterics. She shouldn't have dithered though. It was now five o'clock at home. It might be too late to call any offices. But whatever the case, she needed Eric's thoughts on this

"Well hello, beautiful," Eric said, after one ring, lifting Evelyn's flagging spirits slightly. "I didn't expect to hear from you today. Isn't it pretty late where you are?"

She didn't pass time with the pleasantries. "Eric, did you hear from Child Services? Did you tell them I'd left town by myself instead of us going together?"

"No, why?"

To her dismay, a sob escaped despite her best efforts to talk sense to herself.

"What's happening, sweetheart? Talk to me, you're starting to freak me out."

After a gulping breath, Evelyn pulled herself together enough to explain the email she had received. She also shared her thoughts trying to convince herself it must have been a mistake.

"I agree with you, it can't be correct. It's basically just a matter of weeks before a kid comes to live with us. Everything has been confirmed. Something isn't right. I'm sure it's just a mistake."

"Even if it's a mistake, a mistake like that could eliminate us. Or majorly delay the process. If we have to apply and get approved all over again, who knows how long that will take. Maybe you were right and this is just too much for us."

"Take a breath, Evie. You've come so far in your strength journey. Don't go back to the swamp or whatever you called it. This could all just be a clerical error. I'll call Gloria right now. If I can't get a hold of her this afternoon, I'll do so as soon as her office opens in the morning. Don't worry about this, I'll get it straightened out. I'm sure it's just a mistake."

"Maybe I should call, Eric. I've been the one talking to them most of the time. Maybe it's because I came to France by myself."

"I don't know how they could possibly even know about that, but it's all the more reason for it to be me that calls, don't you think? If they think we're having problems, it might be reassuring for them to hear my side of things."

Evelyn took another shuddering breath and nodded even though Eric couldn't see her. "I see your point. Are you sure you don't mind?"

"Not in the least, sweetheart." Eric took a deep breath. Evelyn could almost hear him willing her to be reasonable. She took another deep breath herself and let it out, calming even further. Before she could say anything else, Eric continued, "Thank you for calling me and sharing this with me. Would you forward me the email so I can read it for myself?"

"Oh, of course, I should have done that right away but I thought you might've gotten it too. Just a sec." She suited her words to action and sent the email to him.

"Thanks. I'll read it through and then I'll call Gloria. We'll get this sorted out. And you should try to get some sleep. It is soon going to be the middle of the night over there, isn't it?"

"I don't think I could sleep until I hear back from you."

"Don't wait up, sweetheart, I know this is just some crossed signals somewhere along the line. You'll be wrecked if you don't get some sleep. And you know how busy Gloria is. I might not be able to make contact with her tonight or even into tomorrow."

Reluctantly Evelyn had to agree. The social worker was extremely busy. A massive yawn overtook her, causing her to chuckle slightly despite her disquiet.

"I guess you're right. But promise you'll call me as soon as you know anything. Don't worry about waking me up. I'm not sure I'll even be able to sleep anyway, so please don't hesitate to call."

"I promise, Evie, as long as you promise to try to get a bit of sleep."

"I promise," Evelyn vowed. "And I love you."

"Love you too. You'll see, this will all get sorted out."

Feeling relieved, minutes later Evelyn drifted off to a fitful sleep.

The restless sleep didn't last too long though as a couple hours later she awoke with a gasp from a nightmare in which she was on the beach by her home in Cape Avalon desperately searching for a missing child. Her stomach hurt, and her throat felt raw from her crying the night before. Even though she was still tired, Evelyn had no interest in staying in bed any longer. She needed some sea therapy. Even though it was still early, it might be soothing to watch the sun rise, she thought with a slight spurt of optimism.

Awake again. Going for a walk. Call or message whenever you'd like.

Evelyn dashed off a quick text message after she washed her face and pulled her hair into a haphazard ponytail despite the fact that Eric would likely be sleeping. She didn't bother with makeup or styling. She wasn't interested in anything fashionable that morning. She needed to walk off her anxiety before she could consider anything else. Hopefully Eric had already found out something helpful and just hadn't wished to disturb her sleep. But he would have messaged her, she was sure, knowing how upset she had been.

She had to hold the railing as she almost ran down the four flights of stairs for fear of being unsteady on her feet, but once she gained the street Evelyn was much more surefooted. Despite being a foreign location, it was already starting to feel like home in an odd way. She had walked around the neighborhood often enough that she knew her way easily without needing to consult her map app. Soon she was stomping along the pebbled beach with the soothing rhythm of the waves comforting her.

She wished she was on the Cape. The familiar sound of the waves crashing on the sand might be even better than this. But still, the rhythmic, rolling rattle settled her nerves and by the time the sky turned to pinks, oranges, and then yellows, Evelyn was feeling much more resolute.

Whatever had happened, they would find a solution. But she should probably go home. While she was fully confident that anything was surmountable, it was better faced side by side with Eric, not with an ocean between them.

She would look into rearranging her flight when she got back to the apartment later. For now, she needed a little more walking to feel fully grounded.

By the time she'd walked at least a couple miles and then stopped for a *petit dejeuner* of *café au lait* and a flaky croissant, Evelyn was feeling much more herself, even though the fact that she still hadn't heard from Eric left her feeling restless. Eric should be getting up soon. Maybe he hadn't been able to reach Gloria the evening before. But how could Gloria not have called him back? Did he not leave a message? Did he not tell her how serious the matter was? Evelyn itched to contact the woman herself, but she had promised Eric to leave it in his capable hands. She needed to do so. It certainly wouldn't do their marriage any good if she didn't keep her word.

But it was hard!

Chapter Eighteen

After a day and a half had gone by, Eric finally called with news.

Evelyn had barely eaten in that time even though she had continued to go through the motions of enjoying her time in France. She had forced herself to go out and practice her French skills even though all she wanted to do was curl up in the armchair and stare at her phone.

She was becoming increasingly comfortable practicing her language skills even though they weren't very acute. Evelyn wondered if part of it was her disquiet. She was so discouraged about the future state of her family planning that she wasn't feeling insecure about anything else. But she also had an inborn need to interact with people and when she could actually make herself understood through her inexperienced French, it filled her with a much-needed sense of accomplishment.

Evelyn had made it to her pastry class despite her inclination to remain isolated. She wasn't sure if she would be able to concentrate on the baking class or be a pleasant companion, but she took the risk and went anyway.

She was glad she did. She was now the proud owner of several *profiteroles*, *cannelles*, and *palmiers*. Well, there wouldn't be much left other than crumbs soon, she thought as she stared at the box she had brought them home in. Had she really eaten that many? Well, not that many. And she had barely eaten all day. But there were always consequences to eating that many carbs in one sitting.

All other thought fled her mind when Eric finally called.

"Eric!" she nearly squealed into the phone. "I've been dying. I didn't want to call and bother you too much so I waited until I heard from you, but I nearly died in the process. Do you know anything?"

"Sorry, babe, I would have called sooner but Gloria had to look into it and she took her sweet time. I can understand you not wanting to harass me, as I was in the same boat of not wanting to blow up Gloria's phone. But you could have totally called me, you know that, anytime."

Evelyn laughed. "I know, but I didn't want us to be depressed together. It was better living in hope, maybe." She laughed again but it was a rather forced, dismal little sound. "So what did she say?"

"She said it was a huge mistake and it has nothing to do with us and that we have nothing to worry about. She promised she'll get it sorted out."

Evelyn started to sob all over again.

"Babe, this is good news, why are you crying?"

"I didn't even realize how worried I was. I was so afraid that, even if it was in error, that it might still ruin our chances."

"Nope, Gloria said she will get it all straightened out and it should be completely stricken from our file. It will just take her some time to get it sorted. She's pretty sure it's just a crossed wire somewhere and she'll sort it out. Maybe a name mix up or something since it was only sent to you."

Evelyn was quiet for a moment, clearly worrying Eric.

"Babe, honey, Evie, talk to me. Are you okay? I'm sure it's all going to be okay."

"Yeah, yes, I'm fine. I'm just worried about how many times this sort of mistake might happen. Like are some people given children that never should have been and other, perfectly competent people, prevented from helping because a mistake was made somewhere along the way?"

Eric's heavy exhale indicated his frustration, and Evelyn almost wished she had kept her thoughts to herself. But they had agreed they would share all their thoughts, always.

"It makes me sick to think about it," Evelyn admitted.

"Don't think about it, then, Evie, since there's nothing we can do about it. We will just have to do the very best we can with whichever children we are blessed with and not think about the ones we can't help."

Evelyn sighed too. "I think I'm going to need to speak with the therapist just to deal with that aspect of it," she admitted with a choked laugh.

"I'll come with you," Eric said immediately.

"Will you really?" Evelyn asked, hope and delight filling her. She dried her tears and felt the future brighten once more.

"Absolutely. I was thinking we should make an appointment for as soon as we're back home."

"Speaking of that," Evelyn began, "I was thinking about getting my ticket changed to come home right now."

There was silence between them for a moment before Eric asked, "Have you done it already?"

"No, I was trying too hard to keep my upset under control that I didn't want to be indoors hunched over my tablet."

"Oh good, because I'm going to be knocking on your door in about sixteen hours. I'm on the way to the airport right now."

"What?" Evelyn squealed. "You're coming? You got a flight? When did you book it?"

Eric's rich chuckle filled her ear. "That's a lot of questions, babe," he said, laughing. "I booked it right before you told me about that strange email. I was actually getting worried I wouldn't hear back from Gloria before I got on my flight. So this was a relief."

Evelyn squealed again. "Give me all the flight details. You're flying into Nice, right? I'll meet you at the airport."

"You don't have to do that. I can just grab a taxi."

"I won't be able to settle into doing anything if I'm waiting for you. I'd rather meet you. And the tram is lots of fun anyway. And you'll never find the apartment without my help, at least not without lots of wandering around. I'll be able to play tour guide. It'll be great."

Eric laughed again. "You aren't going to be able to sleep with all this excitement, are you?"

Evelyn's answering laugh was a little shaky in return. "It's been a rollercoaster of emotions. And I drowned my sorrows in carbs this evening, so I actually think I might sleep really well. If not, I'll take something. I want to have all the energy to show you around."

With just a few more words exchanged, after Evelyn got all Eric's flight information, they ended the call. Evelyn was feeling giddy with relief and excitement over Eric's imminent arrival. Suddenly Evelyn went into a whirl of cleaning to get the small apartment ready for Eric to see it. It hadn't been much to look at from the start, but with a bit of cleaning and tidying it should be presentable enough. Maybe a small bunch of flowers could liven it up and be appealing.

Not that Eric was the sort to take note of such things. Evelyn laughed at herself. She was the one who cared more about the house and how clean everything would be. It wasn't likely Eric would even notice. But Evelyn knew she would feel better if she had done the house cleaning before he turned up.

All the while, Evelyn imagined she had a small child in tow. She pretended she was picking up toys or showing a small boy how to fold the laundry or a little girl how to mop the floors. She shook her head. She was verging on delusional. But she didn't care. She and Eric would soon have a child. Maybe within weeks.

Not maybe, for sure, Evelyn insisted to herself with a sleepy smile as she finally climbed into bed to try to sleep away a few hours before Eric's arrival.

It was going to be so great to have her husband with her in this beautiful place.

That was Evelyn's last thought before she fell into a deep sleep for several hours until waking with a gasp from another nightmare.

It had seemed so realistic. Evelyn knew that it was just the stress of the last couple of days causing it, but it was still difficult to shake the emotions the dream had stirred up. Evelyn refused to give in to tears again, but it took some serious effort to get herself out of the funk the dream left her in.

Why did she have to keep having these visions of losing a child? They hadn't lost any. She had just never managed to get a child yet. They couldn't get pregnant. *She* couldn't get pregnant. But she was done lamenting that part of the past, she reminded herself. They were going in a different direction now. They would have children in their lives. She was nearly convinced of it. They were so close. She could almost feel the child in her arms. She could see herself walking on the beach with him or her, or maybe even more than one. That thought quickly sent her off into a revery of what it would be like to receive siblings into their home. How wonderful to be the means by which those poor darlings could stay together.

It was only the uncertainty that had been stirred up by that email from Child Services. Even though Gloria had assured Eric she would get it straightened out, that still wasn't a sure thing. That was probably what had triggered the nightmare. Until they had a child under their roof, Evelyn wasn't sure if she would be settled on the topic.

But they *were* going to be parents. That was certain. Somehow. Some way.

Thinking these thoughts helped to rid her of the wretched images from her bad dream. But she couldn't go back to sleep. After yawning and stretching, Evelyn got up and ready for her day. Downing the last of the pastries and a bit of yogurt, Evelyn realized she had loads of time left so she decided to walk to the airport. It was several miles, but she had already worked her way up to being ready for it. Besides, if she tired, she could always grab the tram the rest of the way. It would help her settle her excitement about Eric's arrival before she made a fool of herself when welcoming him.

Not that it was foolish to be excited about her husband's arrival. That should be expected, in fact. She hadn't been this excited about seeing Eric since they were kids back in their college days.

But it was a relief when Lucie messaged to arrange to meet for coffee. It would help pass the time and she enjoyed the Frenchwoman's company.

She arrived at the designated appointment and was surprised to find Lucie had her daughter, Sophie, with her.

"You won't mind, Evie, since you are planning for children, no? You can give me advice on what to do with this one."

Evelyn's eyebrows crept toward her hairline as the twelve-year-old girl slouched down in a chair by the window and proceeded to ignore the two women.

"I am, how you would say, in the dog house," Lucie said.

"Why?" Evelyn asked with a light laugh.

"It's not funny," Sophie growled from her place, evidently not ignoring them as much as she implied.

"I'm sorry, I wasn't laughing at you, Sophie. Do you want to talk about it?" Evelyn wasn't sure how to handle the situation. She was clearly far less knowledgeable than she'd like to think.

"She won't let me go to the party. Dad would have let me go, but he had to go away for work." The girl slouched even further.

"It is true, you cannot go, but I don't think your father would have let you go."

"Yes, he would have," Sophie cried loudly.

Lucie looked at Evelyn and rolled her eyes. "This wasn't supposed to be my days to have her. I am thrilled to get to see her more, but I would really like to think her father would not have said "yes" to this invitation. There aren't going to be any parents at this party, so you can be sure there would be drinking. I am not so liberal as to think it's okay for my twelve-year-old daughter to start drinking."

"No, of course not."

"Argh, you are both awful," Sophie nearly screamed, making Evelyn glad they were on the patio instead of inside the café.

"I am sorry, Evelyn, I should not have invited you to join us."

"No, no, this is fine."

They quickly placed their order with the harried server. Sophie deigned to allow them to order a treat for her, but she ignored them other than that despite Evelyn's efforts to draw her into a different topic.

"Perhaps you should be grateful that you don't have an almost teenager in your home," Lucie remarked, and Evelyn couldn't really argue with the thought. Drinking? At that young age? She hadn't thought about those types of problems they might face. And foster children might be even more inclined toward such issues if they came from homes of substance abuse.

Fear clenched in Evelyn's stomach. Maybe Eric had been right to hesitate. Had they been too hasty to get the situation straightened out with Gloria? Was it even straightened out? Turmoil swirled along with the cappuccino in her belly.

"Never mind our troubles, Evelyn, tell us your plans for the day."

A grin forced itself onto Evie's face despite her misgivings. "I'm on the way to the airport to meet my husband."

"*Quoi*? He is coming to join you? *Mais, c'est merveilleux!*"

Evelyn laughed. "I would have to agree."

"Is this a surprise?"

Evelyn nodded happily. "We had originally planned to come together, but something interfered with Eric's plans. Then he was able to rearrange things and he's almost here now."

"So you will have, what? Two weeks here together?"

"I expect so," Evelyn answered. She hadn't really asked Eric about his plans in detail. She had been so relieved that he was coming that she had just assumed it would be for the rest of her stay. She almost shrugged. It didn't really matter. He would be here, that was really all that mattered to her at the moment. She could feel a grin tugging at her mouth.

"Should we take him for a bicycle tour?" Lucie asked.

"I think he would love it, but I'll have to ask him first. I'm not sure how he'll do with jetlag and everything."

"I will text you the schedule and you let me know."

Evelyn was about to say something else but Sophie petulantly interrupted. "Are we almost done here, *Mama*?"

Evelyn looked at her friend as she winced and shook her head in apology. "I am sorry, Evelyn. We must go. Perhaps I shouldn't have bothered you today."

"Not a bother at all, it is a pleasure to see you. I should be on my way to meet Eric anyway. And I was happy to meet you, too, Sophie. I'm sorry that old ladies aren't very interesting for you."

Sophie huffed out a surprised chuckle, obviously not expecting such a sentiment from her mother's friend. Watching her, Evelyn could see she wasn't a bad kid. Really, there weren't likely to be any bad kids. Just misguided or misdirected ones. It was an encouraging thought. Because watching the young girl have a meltdown had most definitely not been encouraging to her and her future plans.

"Thank you for the visit," Lucie said, getting to her feet. "But I probably need to get this one somewhere else."

Evelyn grinned. "And I have a flight to meet. I will see you soon, I hope." With airy kisses to the cheeks, the women took their leave of one another. Evelyn's feet were light as she hurried on her way.

Chapter Nineteen

velyn managed to walk the entire way to the airport and was still a few minutes early for Eric's flight. She wouldn't have expected so with stopping for the coffee with Lucie. She had walked briskly. But her success was only due to his flight being delayed by forty-five minutes, though, so she shouldn't feel smug about it. She also might regret it later when she was falling asleep far too early in the evening, but then again, if he wasn't able to sleep on the plane, Eric would be tired really early, too, so maybe it was a good thing.

She was babbling nervously, even in her own mind, Evelyn realized with a roll of her eyes. There was absolutely no reason to be nervous. Eric was on his way to her. That clearly meant they were fine, or would be. She wanted them to be. He must want them to be. They were reasonably intelligent adults. They could make it happen.

With or without children, she insisted to herself with a lift of her chin. That was the whole point. She was done mourning. Yes, she would always have a sliver of grief in her heart where their birth children ought to be, but that was fine.

Together, she and Eric would find a way to have a successful, fulfilling life together. They would decide, together, what that was supposed to look like, and then they would make it happen. Starting with this time in France. Evelyn didn't want to wait until some other tragedy happened before they took a spectacular trip together. Really, travel was such an enriching experience, it ought to be a regular part of their lives.

With or without children, she thought again with a grin.

If their travel was to be with children, then it might involve a theme park or two, in addition to views and museums, but children's lives needed to be enriched, as well. It was part of their education.

Of course, with a social worker, it was likely they would need permission to take any foster children on travels, but that was fine too. Raising children by committee would only be to the children's benefit, surely. How did biological parents do it, with no one with any experience?

And there he was. With a squeal she couldn't prevent, Evelyn launched herself into Eric's waiting arms. It felt to her as though it had been months since she'd seen him in the flesh rather than barely two weeks. But she supposed that was down to the growth and changes she felt she had made. Evelyn felt as though she were a different person. Eric would have to get to know her all over again.

"What has you grinning so mischievously?" Eric asked with a quirk of his eyebrow.

"I was just thinking that you might find me a little different than before," Evelyn explained. "I'm amused at the anticipation I feel over how you might react to the changes."

Eric pulled her tighter in response. "I look forward to it," he answered with a smile as he smothered her in kisses.

"*Les Americains*," someone said with a drawl of amusement, passing by them, making Evelyn laugh out loud.

"Let's get your suitcase and get out of here. We're going to give the French a toothache or a heart attack with our public displays of affection."

"Really?" Eric asked, laughing. "I would have thought the French would be far less uptight than us."

Evelyn shrugged. "You'd think so, but I guess they don't make allowances for those of us of advanced age."

Eric's chuckle in her ear was her reward for her wit. "Here, you stand out of the crowd, I'll just go grab my bag and we can get out of here."

Evelyn nodded as she accepted his backpack from him so he could maneuver more freely through the crowds. Within minutes they were slipping out of the terminal.

"I know you've been loving living like a local but after all those flights, I think I'd rather wait a day or two before I start walking all over the place," Eric said in a cajoling tone as Evelyn was heading for the tram station. She quickly adjusted her direction.

"No problem. We'll grab a cab. But you will have to walk part of the way since our apartment is in the pedestrian zone."

"I can see it has been agreeing with you," Eric said with admiration as he took in her slimmed down physique. Evelyn merely answered with a grin.

"How are you holding up? Were you able to sleep at all on your flights?"

"There was a couple screaming children sitting near me on the transatlantic flight, so not much," Eric replied with a crooked smile. "But now that I'm with you, I feel energized."

Evelyn leaned in for a quick kiss for that bit of flummery, happy to have butterflies of excitement fluttering in her tummy.

"So let's drop off your bags and I'll show you around. If we can keep you up for a few more hours, we'll be able to beat most of your jetlag."

"I'll follow your lead, captain," Eric answered with a saluting gesture and a laugh.

"When's the last time you ate?"

Eric laughed. "Parts of you might have changed, but obviously the part that needs to look after everyone is still alive and well."

Evelyn returned his grin with a sheepish one of her own, but merely shrugged in response.

The afternoon and evening flew by with Evelyn towing Eric around to every one of her favorite spots in the old part of Nice. They finally stopped to eat at a lovely patio overlooking the sea across the street from the promenade.

"You've really made good use of your time, I can tell," Eric complimented. "Not only have you walked yourself into physical shape but you really seem lighter somehow in a figurative way. Like you aren't weighed down by cares and concerns anymore."

Evelyn nodded, looking out at the ceaseless waves.

"I seem to have been able to get a grip in the last two weeks. While I can't say I appreciated your sending me here alone when it happened, I also can't say that it hasn't been a really great experience. Having solitary time to just be silent and think through everything seems to have done me a world of good. And stepping out of my comfort zone has been a learning and growing experience that I'll always appreciate having."

"I'm so glad. And I'm thrilled you aren't holding a grudge," Eric said, tightening his grip on her hand where it lay on the table.

"Grudges are such a waste of energy," Evelyn said with a wink. "I burned off that energy climbing the Castle Hill." She paused and wiggled her eyebrows. "Speaking of which, I'm really hoping you will have the energy to do that climb in the morning. It has the best views. And I think I've figured out where our apartment is from up there so I want to be able to point it out to you. It's kind of bragging, but I don't even care."

Eric threw back his head and chortled. Evelyn loved the carefree sound of it and felt contentment settle into the soles of her feet.

"I still think we should go see a therapist when we go home. I think there are more issues we ought to face," Evelyn said, hoping she wasn't about to spoil their beautiful moment.

"I agree."

"Really? Just like that?"

"Yeah, just like that," Eric said with a low laugh. "Or rather, seeing how resilient you've turned out to be, maybe I want some of that too. But I don't think Nice is going to do it for me like it has for you."

Evelyn laughed too. "Maybe not. But I also think it would be good for us to figure out a good form of communication. We shouldn't have gotten to the place we did. While I'm thrilled that we survived the swamp of despair, and I'm willing to go through it with you again, I'd really rather we don't."

"No swamps for us. So that's a 'yes' for therapy, then."

Evelyn grinned, the bubble of contentment rising from her soles to encompass all of her. For some reason, she felt as though Eric were holding something back but she dismissed the thought. She was just being paranoid. They were far too happy to be keeping secrets from one another at this point.

***

Several blissful days passed in which Evelyn showed Eric all her favorite spots in the beautiful southern city. They hiked and climbed as much as she wanted but they also went further afield too, renting a car for a few days and exploring other parks and cities she hadn't been able to get to on her own.

It had been a pleasure to see Eze again, even if she couldn't walk all the way home as had been her intention if she had gone alone a second time, but she had been thrilled when Eric had agreed to hike the coastal trail with her to the lighthouse in Cap Ferrat after they had spent a few days in the car.

Despite Evelyn's newfound love of walking, even she had to admit the Calanques and the hills around Marseille had been worth driving to see.

One evening, after they'd accompanied Lucie on one of her bike-riding winery tours, they held hands as they strolled along the promenade just as the sun was going down. Evelyn again felt very aware of her contentment as she breathed deeply of the fresh air coming in off the bay with the warmth of the setting sun on her face and her much loved husband at her side.

That contentment was threatened, though, when Eric's grip on her hand tightened convulsively and his face turned serious as he leaned toward her. But not serious in a good way. She couldn't explain it but for a brief moment she wanted to run away. She didn't want to hear whatever he was about to tell her. She didn't know why, it felt instinctive.

"I have to tell you something," Eric began. Evelyn almost pulled her hand out of his grip but he held on and then so did she after swallowing convulsively.

She wouldn't allow her mind to run to all the negative possibilities. That wasn't her anymore, she reminded herself despite the instincts that pervaded. Dredging up a smile, Evelyn looked her husband in the eye and nodded. "I'm lulled into a sense of comfort with good food, great company, and the warmth of the setting sun," she said with a light laugh. "What do you need to tell me?"

"Gloria still hasn't gotten the fostering matter cleared up. It might be because she knows we're away so it isn't on the top of her priority list. I don't know. But there is a slight possibility this mix up is turning out to be more challenging to correct than she expected."

Evelyn stared at her husband and mentally tried to assess how she was feeling. She had told herself that children or no children she would be fine. Had she lied to herself? No, with a lift of her chin, Evelyn kept her gaze steady on Eric.

"Well then, we'd best have a wonderful vacation, hadn't we?" she finally said. It didn't matter that the two statements weren't exactly matching. The fact was that she had worked so hard for the last three weeks on being able to face whatever the future might hold. She wasn't going to allow Eric's statement to ruin her delight in having him with her in France and all that they were determined to do, together, as a couple.

"You're taking this remarkably well," Eric said with a slight frown.

"Would you prefer hysterics? I could muster them for you, if you'd like. But I would prefer to wait until we have some privacy for that," she added with as light a laugh as she could muster.

Eric chuckled. "Of course not. I was just worried about telling you."

"The whole point of this trip was to come to terms with our barrenness and reach a place of cooperation between the two of us, right?" At Eric's nod, Evelyn continued, "I've tried really hard to accept what is. While, yes, I had thought we'd be welcoming children into our lives in some form, if that won't happen, I know now that I'll be okay."

"Wow, Evie, that's great." Eric said before he ran a hand through his hair. "But Gloria did have another idea she thought we ought to consider. She told me about it just before I flew over here, but I wasn't sure if I should tell you about it. It's different. Better in some ways, in my opinion, but bringing a different set of complications. I've been thinking about it all week, and I really think it could be the best thing for us." At her continued silence, and maybe because of her slight frown, Eric hurried to continue explaining himself. "I know I should have told you right away, but I really thought we would have heard from Gloria by now about fostering so I didn't want to bring this other option into the mix. But now, I really think we should think about it."

Fear and anticipation clenched Evelyn's stomach and she stared at her husband expectantly when he didn't continue right away. Her lifted eyebrows must have prompted him as he continued with a nervous smile.

"I thought we had agreed to open communication, Eric. You shouldn't have been worrying about this by yourself for days."

"You're right. I'm sorry," he said, before blurting, "Have you heard of open adoptions?"

"Of course, I've heard of them," Evelyn said. "That's where you adopt a child but the mother or maybe even both biological parents stay in your and the child's lives at some level, right?"

"Yes, exactly," Eric said, eagerly, leaning toward her and squeezing her hand. "What do you think of it?"

Evelyn opened her mouth to answer but then realized she ought to think it through a little more. She lifted a shoulder in a helpless shrug.

"I'm not really sure what to think of it, honestly. You tell me what you think of it, since you've obviously had a little more time to give it thought than I have."

A nervous expression flitted across Eric's face, followed by a look of determination.

"Maybe I should have waited until we went home," Eric started despite that determination.

"Nonsense," Evelyn countered immediately. "We're solid, Eric, you know that. And I swear to you, I'm okay. Nothing you can say will make that not true."

"Wow, you really have come a long way in these weeks."

Evelyn laughed but gestured for him to continue, not wanting to get sidetracked. Eric cleared his throat and started to talk. "Okay. Here's the thing. I know you thought adoption would take too long, isn't that why you thought we should go with fostering?"

Evelyn waggled her head, not sure if she was agreeing or disagreeing. "Sort of. I also think all those little ones could use a good home."

"Of course, but don't you think it would be better to get one we can keep?"

Evelyn laughed. "Yes, I do like permanence."

"Exactly. While I agreed with you about fostering, and I know we could do some good in these kids' lives, I just don't know if my heart has the resilience needed to bear up under the tragedies we would be forced to witness in their lives. If we have to let them go back to situations we can't fix for them, I just don't know how we would do it."

"I believe we would be comforted by knowing we had done the best for them we could while we had them," Evelyn began, but then added, "I know it wouldn't be easy, though. And you're right, our hearts will break multiple times, I'm sure. But I believe we have what it takes. I think our hearts have all the resiliency needed. Even broken hearts mend again and again."

"But what if there's another option?"

"You're talking about open adoption, now, right?"

"Yeah," Eric said eagerly. "What if there's some teenager out there who could use our help. She'd give us her baby to raise. In exchange we could help her too."

"You might be putting a fanciful spin on it," Evelyn warned.

"Maybe, but that's kind of the way Gloria presented it to me," Eric said with a little laugh.

"I'm surprised; she's struck me as being almost too realistic. Are you sure that's not just what you wanted to hear from her?" Evelyn tried to ask the question as gently as she could, but it was still a rather harsh thing to say.

To her relief, Eric just grinned and shook his head even as he pointed to a café on the other side of the road. "Should we go grab a drink and talk about this? Or maybe go back to the apartment? I know you are great at walking and talking but I find it a bit distracting."

"Sure," Evelyn replied promptly, changing direction. "Let's go back to the apartment. I have a nice red that might go down well with this discussion."

They quickly found themselves back in the small apartment. Since Eric had arrived, they'd only been there for sleeping and breakfast, but it was cute and cozy enough for their evening conversation.

Their knees were nearly touching in the small space as they sat down with their glasses, facing each other, but that was probably a good thing. They were in this together; they needed the physical reminder of that sometimes.

"So have you heard from Gloria since you've been here? Or is this all based on the conversation you had before coming?" Evelyn began.

"I just got an update email from her this afternoon saying she was still working on the fostering mix-up but that she had some pregnant moms who might be interested in us. If we give her the go ahead, she'll show them our file even though we haven't filled out the official forms for open adoption."

Evelyn stared at her husband for a couple of beats, processing his words. "I find myself wondering why you didn't bring this up as soon as you got here, since she obviously presented you with that idea days ago." Evelyn wasn't mad, but she was a little hurt or worried or something. Why hadn't he brought it up?

Eric sighed. "You were in such a good place, Evie. I didn't want to rock that. But I really want to give her the go ahead to talk to those moms, so I couldn't put it off any longer."

Evelyn laughed a little even though she wasn't really amused. "It's a good thing we agreed to go to therapy together when we get home because obviously communication is still an issue."

"You're right, Eve, I'm sorry. I should have shared this right away."

"So you've thought it through and you think this is a good idea?" Evelyn asked.

Eric still appeared sheepish but he nodded eagerly.

"Tell me why," Evelyn invited, keeping her body language open, not folding her arms even though that was a position of comfort for her. She knew it would put her husband on the defensive, and that was the last thing she wanted. It was just that talking about babies made her emotional despite how far she'd come in her personal journey.

"Like I told you, even though you think it sounds a little like a fairy tale, I think the possibility of helping out the birth mom *and* having a child to call our own would kind of combine both things we were hoping for, you know?" Eric said eagerly. "Like you wanted to take in foster kids to help out needy kids, right." At her nod, he explained. "Well, if a mom needs to give up her baby, surely, she's in the greater need, wouldn't you say?"

"But what if she changes her mind?" Evelyn asked.

"That, or worse, could happen with fostering. It's actually kind of the point of fostering, really. To give the kid back."

"Yeah, but we're going into that expecting it, you know what I mean? Like we know fostering is temporary. There's no expectation that we can keep the child. How will we cope if we go through a pregnancy with a girl or woman, set our heart on the child, and then she decides when the baby is born that she's changed her mind?"

Eric sighed heavily, raking his hand through his hair. "I know, Evie, that's probably a possibility. In fact, I think they have a few months to change their mind. But isn't it worth the risk? You were willing, for years, to put yourself through so many medical experiments with the hopes of having a baby. And we still don't have one. Isn't this worth taking a chance on?"

Evelyn sighed too but kept herself leaning forward, open to conversation with her husband. "It might be. Yes, of course, it would be worth it. But what about the fostering?"

"Do you think, maybe we should go ahead with both? Like keep Gloria trying to get the denial reversed, but tell her to go ahead and show our information to the moms she's currently thinking of? Maybe we could get started on whatever the application process is right away?"

Evelyn laughed. "Hedge our bets, then, is that what you're suggesting?" She shook her head. "I thought we had agreed not to have our hopes up anymore."

"That was on biological children, not children all together."

Suddenly, Evelyn's heart soared and she fought the prickle of tears behind her eyes. "You're right, Eric. If there's a chance we might be able to have a baby, even if it's not one of our own, we should try for it. Yes, tell Gloria to show our information to whoever she thinks might be a right fit. And let's look at what else we need to do."

Eric grabbed her glass from her hand, put his down next to hers on the table, and then pulled her from her chair, twirling her gently around the small room, managing not to knock any furniture over in the process.

"Thank you, babe. You won't regret this."

They rejoiced together for the rest of their night, but at some point, before slipping into deep sleep, Evelyn noted the glow of Eric's cellphone.

"What are you doing?"

"It's just after business hours at home, Gloria might get my email tonight if I send it now."

Evelyn chuckled and shook her head even as she drifted off to sleep.

Chapter Twenty

With no desire to brood, Evelyn dragged Eric out of the apartment after a fortifying breakfast of eggs, fruit, fresh baguette, and strong coffee.

"You're exceedingly efficient in this small space," Eric had complimented. "After two weeks of fending for myself, I'm all the more grateful for your culinary skills."

Evelyn just offered a cheeky grin in response, even as she hurried him from the small space. "Let's get going. I want to show you my favorite views in Eze today. We have a bus to catch." She paused for a second before adding, "It's the middle of the night over there. We can't expect to hear from Gloria for hours yet, if even today. You know how busy she is."

"I know, you're right," Eric nodded. "Lead the way."

They both enjoyed their day, but Evelyn knew they were each thinking about what could possibly await them at home. After Eric's revelations the night before, Evelyn's heart wasn't in France any longer. She longed to be in their own cozy but spacious beach home, staring out at her own familiar surf. Better yet, she longed to be taking whatever steps were necessary to try out this new option that had been presented to them.

"I'm not sorry you waited to tell me, though," Evelyn blurted as she was pointing out a particularly beautiful view to Eric. He didn't even blink, knowing exactly what she was talking about despite how off topic it was from where they were.

"I'm glad we've had this week together, too," Eric agreed immediately.

"Now that I know, I'll admit I'm a little over being here."

Eric laughed. "I know what you mean. But rushing home isn't going to change anything."

"It might."

Eric laughed again. "Your go-getter personality is always so focused. I thought you were learning to live in the moment."

Evelyn cleared her throat and nodded, turning back to the view. "You're right. We shouldn't waste this glorious day on worries, either good or bad."

They stood in silence for a few minutes, taking it all in.

"But we should have talked about my career. We didn't do that yet," Evelyn blurted again, a new thought this time.

"What do you mean?" Eric asked, turning to her with a puzzled frown.

"Remember, we talked about it a couple weeks ago. I want to get a career idea. I'd like to have it in place as soon as possible so that it can support our life with children rather than interfere."

Eric nodded encouragingly, turning his back on the majestic vista to give his wife his full attention. "Have you come up with any ideas?"

Evelyn grinned. "Well, to be honest, I've been having too much fun to give it any truly serious thought, but what do you think of me opening a virtual assistant business?"

"What does a virtual assistant do?" Eric asked, sounding curious, not dismissive.

"From what I can tell, he or she does whatever I am able to do. Since I have so much experience as an executive assistant, it might be right in my wheelhouse. And it would give me control over my schedule and workload. I can limit myself to as many clients as I think I can comfortably handle."

"Where would you find your clients?" Eric asked, again, sounding supportive, but wondering.

"Well, I could reach out to my old firm and see if they wanted to freelance out some tasks. That would be the easiest. But something Rachel said had me thinking in a different direction. She said all of her author friends could use a few hours per week or per month help with all the nitpicky tasks they'd rather not do themselves. You know nitpicky is right up my alley."

Eric laughed and nodded. "It is, but only in the very best way."

Evelyn put her arm around her husband and leaned into his strength.

"What would go into opening a virtual assistant business? Have you thought about that?"

Evelyn nodded. "I have, yes. Basically, all I'd need is a website. And maybe a PayPal account, or something similar, to bill my clients. It's pretty simple. I just have to decide what exactly I want to offer as my services and then set my prices. And then get all that up on my website."

Eric laughed. "Despite thinking you hadn't given it enough thought, you seem to have it all figured out."

Evelyn giggled along with him. "Not really, the services and prices are kind of the whole deal, don't you think?"

Eric shrugged. "Maybe, but it's just details. You just need to research what others charge. You can even make it up or change it as you go, seems to me."

Evelyn sighed happily and faced her husband. "Should we grab some lunch? It's getting late and suddenly I'm starving."

Before they made it very far, though, the sound of Eric's phone receiving an email notification paused them in their tracks. Exchanging twin expressions of trepidation with Eric, Evelyn felt both excited anticipation and dread sweeping through her. A quick glance at her watch told her it wasn't even nine o'clock in the morning back home. Was this good news or bad?

Dear Eric and Evelyn,

I'm sorry to say that I can't figure out where the glitch came in on your fostering application so we're going to have to resubmit if you want to go forward in that direction. The good news is, we don't have to redo the home inspection or classes, just the actual application, so it should only take a few more weeks. Let me know and I'll send you the forms again. Or you might already have the originals, just change the dates and send it back to me, if you do.

As for the open adoption, I hope you don't mind. I was so sorry about the fostering mishap and I was so sure you'd be interested that I took the liberty of telling two of my moms about you. I didn't show them anything yet, I wanted to wait for your permission, but I told them all about you and they'd both like to learn more. So, if you want to go forward, I'll show them everything I've got while you get yourselves back here so you can meet them.

Safe travels,

Gloria

Evelyn squealed and started skipping even though it wasn't even that positive of a message.

"Eric! Two moms. Could we get two babies?"

"Slow down, Evie," Eric said with a laugh. "Let's not get ahead of ourselves."

"No, of course not. I don't know if I can eat now, but we should try. Let's keep going to that restaurant I told you about, and I'll try to keep my feet on the ground and my head from the clouds."

"I'm so happy that you're happy about this, Evie. I'm surprised you aren't offended that she talked about us without waiting for our agreement."

Evelyn shrugged. "What harm would that do? I'm just glad we have a social worker in our corner that's trying to do her best for everyone concerned."

Neither of them were in much the mood for eating at that point, but they did manage to split one of the Niçoise special pizzas. They tried to speak of other things and admire the views and chat with their server but it was obvious to both of them they were fully distracted.

"Let's go home," Evelyn said suddenly as they were walking down the steep hill toward the bus stop.

"Isn't that where we're heading?"

"No, let's go home to Cape Avalon. Email Gloria to show whoever whatever and we'll be home in a day or two to complete whatever paperwork is necessary. You know neither of us are going to get anything more out of being here with this hanging over us."

Eric's rich chuckle flowed over her even as he pulled her in for a celebratory kiss. "I'll race you," he called, pushing her forward and running after her down the hill.

Before she could catch her breath, they were back at their apartment, online with the airline, moving their flights forward a couple days. Laughing and singing like little kids anticipating a special treat, Evelyn and Eric made all the arrangements.

Within hours, they had authorized Gloria to share their information with the pregnant women she thought might be a good fit for them as well as received Gloria's files on the two young mothers. They had also found and adjusted the foster parent applications they had previously completed, forwarding them back to Gloria to refresh that process.

"There's plenty of room in my heart," Evelyn had pointed out to Eric. "I think we ought to keep ourselves open to both options."

With everything filled out and sent off and their new departure time settled, Eric smiled down into his wife's upturned face.

"Since we'll be leaving in a day and a half, we'd best get back out there and absorb as much as we can," Eric said.

"Would you like to learn how to make croissants?" Evelyn asked suddenly. "And then you can meet my cooking class friends," she added. "You already met Lucie when we went winery biking. If we leave right now, we can just make it for her class."

"Let's go, then," Eric agreed immediately.

Their steps were light and there was joy in their hearts as Evelyn and Eric stepped out into their future. They were ready for the adventure that lay ahead.

The End

- - - - - - - - - - - - - - -

If you enjoyed Evelyn and Eric's story,
consider reading about their friends.

Return to Sandpiper Cottage

is the first book in the *Cape Avalon* Series.

The Cape Avalon books

are Ms. Andrews' first contemporary set stories.
If you're interested in reading her Historical Romance
fiction, visit the Historical Books page on her website
at www.wendymayandrews.com to learn more.

About the Author

I learned to read when I was four or five, listening to my mother read to me when I was lonely after my brother started school. Ever since, I've had my head buried in books. I love words – historical plaques, signs, the cereal box – but my first love has always been novels.

Nearly fifteen years ago my husband dared me to write a book instead of always reading them. I didn't think I'd be able to do it, but to my surprise I love writing. Those early efforts eventually became my first published book – *Tempting the Earl* (originally published by Avalon Books in 2010). It has been a thrilling adventure as I learned to navigate the world of publishing.

I believe firmly that everyone deserves a happily ever after. I want my readers to be able to escape from the everyday for a little while and feel upbeat and refreshed when they get to the end of my books.

When not reading or writing, I can be found traipsing around my neighbourhood or travelling the world with my favourite companion.

Stay in touch with W. M. Andrews
and all her upcoming publishing news

Sign up for her biweekly newsletter on
www.wendymayandrews.com

Search for "Wendy May Andrews" on:
Google   Facebook   Instagram
TikTok   YouTube

Other books by Wendy May Andrews

The *Cape Avalon* books are Ms. Andrews' first contemporary set stories.

If you're interested in reading her Historical Romance fiction, visit the books page on her website to learn more.

Consider starting her latest series – Northcott Kinship.

Intriguing Lord Adelaide

She's a wallflower debutante—and his best friend's sister. But one dance could change everything.

See the entire collection!

Scan the QR code below